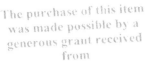

Confessions of a First Daughter

Confessions of a First Daughter

Cassidy Calloway

HARPER TEEN
An Imprint of HarperCollins Publishers

Library of Congress Cataloging-in-Publication Data
Calloway, Cassidy.
  Confessions of a First Daughter / Cassidy Calloway. — 1st ed.
    p. cm.
  Summary: High school senior Morgan Abbott pretends to be her mother, the
President of the United States, as a decoy, while she also tries to lead the life of a
normal teenager.
  ISBN 978-0-06-172439-8
  [1. Presidents—Family—Fiction. 2. Dating (Social customs)—Fiction. 3. High
schools—Fiction. 4. Schools—Fiction.] I. Title.
PZ7.C13457Co 2009   2009001402
[Fic]—dc22   CIP
                                                                                 AC

Typography by Michelle Gengaro-Kokmen
09 10 11 12 13   CG/RRDH   10 9 8 7 6 5 4 3 2 1
❖
First Edition

To Megan and Morgan Thie—Dream big and laugh often!

With special thanks to Kathleen Bolton

Confessions of a First Daughter

Chapter One

I wonder if my mother ever feels like throwing up before she delivers an important speech.

Breathe. Swallow nausea.

Just. Breathe.

I clutched the stage curtain to steady myself and poked my head out so I could scan the empty auditorium. I wasn't prepared to take center stage just yet. I pulled back, telling myself that I wasn't making the State of the Union address beamed by satellite to seventy-four countries including the Antarctic Research Station (annual budget $17.5 million to study the effects of global warming on penguin migratory patterns). Nor was I laying the equivalent of a diplomatic smackdown to a terrorist warlord. My speech before the Academy of the Potomac's student body wouldn't be enshrined in the Smithsonian Institution next to Lincoln's top hat and Prince's electric guitar. I'm not running for president of the United States. My mom already has that job.

But right now getting elected senior class president seemed a lot more difficult.

And Mom's opponent had been the aw-shucks governor of Wyoming. She didn't have to deal with running against Practically Perfect Brittany Whittaker.

Backstage lounging in a chair, "Brits," as her fawning posse calls her, was coolly examining her Wetslicked lips in a jeweled Chanel compact. Snapping the mirror shut, she picked an invisible piece of lint from her designer suit, which was in a tasteful shade of charcoal, of course.

I really wished I'd listened to my best friend, Hannah, when she suggested shopping for a new outfit. But I was too busy stressing out over this speech and greeting the new Mongolian ambassador with Mom and Dad to shop.

Now I looked like my grandma dressed in a basic black suit that the White House's social secretary picked up for me at Staid Fashions or something. It didn't even fit. But I guess that's why safety pins were invented.

I tucked my hair behind my ears. It looked boring, too. I'd let it return to its natural shade of mud brown instead of the magenta I'd been experimenting with. In politics, it's important to look as neutral as possible. Someone might have a prejudice against magenta, after all.

Out front, I could hear chairs grumbling and students chatting as the herd entered the auditorium and took their seats.

It sucks to have to make a speech to a group that's basically being forced to hear it. It sucks even more when they're waiting for you to screw it up, just to enliven another bleak afternoon at AOP. After three years, my classmates know they can count on me to provide regular entertainment value on the goober front.

Well, not this time. No, sir. Morgan Abbott has her game down today.

Be prepared. It's my mom's favorite mantra, and for once I listened to her. I made a list of the things that could go wrong, and then came up with a Plan B. The secretary of state taught me that little trick.

Plan B Checklist

- Gym shorts under my skirt (in case the safety pins keeping my skirt around my waist give out).
- Spare notecards in pocket. (Who could forget the mishap in my sophomore year, when I'd forgotten my notecards and had to babble aimlessly for three minutes?)
- Vocal cords limbered. (Those voice-projection exercises from drama class will pay off if the microphone goes on the fritz.)
- Key points scribbled on hand (in case Plans A and B wash out and I go blank).

Yep. Nothing's going wrong today.

Mrs. Hsu, the principal, tapped me on the shoulder. "We're ready to begin, Morgan."

"Great. Fine. Let's get this party started."

Mrs. Hsu gave me a funny look. "You're not going to be sick, are you?"

"Maybe later," I told her.

"That's the spirit, kiddo," she answered absently as we walked over to Brittany. "Brittany? Ready, hon?"

"Of course." Brittany eased out of her chair like a cat stretching in the sun. "You look really lovely today, Mrs. Hsu. That red is the perfect shade for you."

"Oh? You think so?" Mrs. Hsu smoothed the front of her dress, the one she'd probably been teaching in since 1982, and gave Brittany a wide smile. "Would you like to go first? I'm sure Morgan wouldn't mind."

Mrs. Hsu looked at me.

"Do you?" she asked.

"Uh, no. Guess not," I said, even though I was dying to get my speech over with.

Brittany's pink-frosted smirk should have alerted me to the fact that her feral mind had kicked into action. But right then I was crazy-busy reviewing the points of the three-tiered platform my father had helped me develop. We took our cues from the presentations he used to give when he was the CEO of

Abbott Technology. He'd made Abbott Technology number 312 among the Fortune 500 companies, so he must've been doing something right.

The bullet points on my notecards, which I'd rewritten last night after stupidly losing my originals, flashed through my mind:

- **Improved Academics**
  Lobby for more courses designed to improve SAT scores, which will carry more weight on college applications
- **Positive School Environment**
  A proposed World Cultures Celebration Day (Hannah and I could do our Bollywood dance routine in front of the school)
- **Diverse Social Opportunities**
  More community outreach projects. Recycling soda cans in the cafeteria isn't the only way we can help right here in the nation's capital—volunteering to read to kids at the D.C. library's annual literacy drive is one of countless things we can do.

Brittany and I walked onto the stage, where we took our seats. The auditorium's microphone squealed painfully over Mrs. Hsu's request for everyone to get settled. I glanced over at Special Agent Denny Kublinski, standing in the corner of the auditorium, stage left. Even from here, I could tell that the Venti-sized macchiato he downed at lunch, his third of the day, was making him jittery. It seemed like his Starbucks addiction had increased proportionally with the time he spent assigned to me. As Denny scanned the crowd, his face held no emotion, but I knew he had to be bored out of his mind.

As I stared out at the sea of faces, a flash of electric blue caught my eye. Hannah, never the wallflower, wore her Anna Sui silk mini with boots dyed a matching neon shade. She tossed the Foxy Brown Afro she was sporting this week and gave me a thumbs-up. I wished she could give me some of her legendary self-confidence. Hannah takes crap from no one, not even the president's daughter. I think that's what I love most about her. That and her maniacal urges to make me over à la a *Fix This Hot Mess* reality show. It's fun being her guinea pig.

We both know I need all the help I can get.

I searched the back of the auditorium where the jocks were known to hang. Sure enough, there was my boyfriend, Konner, doing a fist-bump with one of his basketball buds. He ran a hand through his mane of blond hair, and my stomach flip-flopped. Last week his hair was slicked back and he was all Mr. GQ. This week he was controlled mayhem. I'm fully aware Konner's the hottest guy at AOP. His going out with me mystified the entire school, myself included.

Konner got his cell out and began speed texting. I willed

him to look up—I needed a little moral support right now—but his eyes never left the phone's screen.

"Testing, testing," Mrs. Hsu said over the shriek of the AV system. "I want to remind everyone that voting takes place tomorrow morning in the cafeteria. Now we'll hear from our two fine candidates for senior class president. Candidates, you each have five minutes to address your constituents. Brittany, you're first."

Adrenaline surged through me. *Here we go.*

Brittany glided to the podium and gracefully lowered the microphone to the level of her mouth.

Blah, blah, giggle, happy to be given this amazing opportunity, obligatory brownnosing . . . I tuned Brittany out as I feverishly went over my bullet points for the millionth time. Improved Academics. Positive School Environment. Diverse Social Opportunities.

"Here it is"—Brittany's voice rose as if she were about to announce the winner of *American Idol*—"my platform, my Sweet Strategy for Success. . . ."

A dozen of Brittany's posse members, wearing hot-pink T-shirts, started handing out chocolate bars. Hannah took one and let it dangle between her finger and thumb as if it were radioactive plutonium. She held it up for me to see.

My eyes zeroed in on the acid-pink custom wrapper. Huge, black block lettering blared:

IMPROVED ACADEMICS

POSITIVE SCHOOL ENVIRONMENT

DIVERSE SOCIAL OPPORTUNITIES

The realization of what had happened ran me over like a Jeep Wrangler.

Omigod.

Brittany Whittaker had stolen my election platform.

Chapter Two

Of course! How could I have been such a moron?

The incident in AOP's tech center yesterday flashed through my mind: Brittany and a trio of her minions knocking over my backpack; her insincere apologies while helping me pick up the mess. She'd even complimented my choice of T-shirt that day: Kung-Fu Hamster.

Hadn't I learned from my mother to expect, even plan for, dirty tricks in politics? But there's a difference between shady antics and outright theft.

I listened in horror to Brittany's honey-glazed voice ooze all over *my* platform.

"My first Sweet Strategy—I call it the Godiva—is to lobby the school's administration to offer more courses designed to improve SAT scores, which will carry more weight on college applications. Not everyone is Ivy League material. They need all the help they can get." Here she glanced over to where I sat, frozen, and gave me a pitying look through her perfectly Maybellined lashes.

Out in the audience, I saw Hannah's jaw sag. Even she couldn't believe Brittany's blatant thievery, and Hannah was the one who called Brittany the evil love child of Lord Voldemort and June Cleaver.

Mentally, I IM'ed her:

CookieMonster: *OMGAAAWD!!! Whatamigonna do?*
Fashionista: *Dunno. U got more notecards?*

Obviously, the answer was a big fat NO.

Brittany sailed on. "Our school environment is also important. Security is *such* a concern these days. And in Washington, D.C., it's true that certain *special people* have their own Secret Service agent. But ordinary people like *you* and *me* have the right to safety that's not at the expense of the taxpayer."

Over on stage left, Denny adjusted his earpiece. I doubted he realized he was about to become a major obstacle to my election to class president.

Numb, I listened to Brittany finish delivering my platform to the entire senior class, even down to the World Cultures Celebration Day. Mrs. Hsu beamed at her and Brittany blushed when the auditorium erupted into applause and whistles. Her bubblegum posse chanted her name and then tossed Hershey's Kisses in the air to renewed cheers.

You know that moment when you realize that everything in your life has been leading to one point? A point at which you could either blow it big-time or rise to the challenge? This was my moment:

Class president or class dork.

Gracefully, Brittany sat down next to me and demurely folded her manicured hands together.

"Top that, fat ass," she hissed. "Not even Mommy President can save you now."

My scathing comeback to Brittany would have to wait. Brits had just given me an idea. Think: WWPAD—What Would President Abbott Do? I rose and approached the lectern. Mrs. Hsu was having a tough time getting the room to settle down, but the Hershey's Kisses helped as people started to stuff their faces.

I set my notecards on the podium, unclipped the mic, and moved to the edge of the stage. I'd watched my mom do this hundreds of times. Talk to people like they are your friends. Talk *with* them, not *at* them. And *open with a joke . . .*

"Let's give Brittany a round of applause for bringing the treats, folks. I know the chicken parm served in the cafeteria today skirted the line between food and science experiment."

Laughter, a scattering of claps.

I took a deep breath. "Look, you and I know the deal. You're expecting me to stand up here and give you a bunch of campaign promises that have been focus-grouped to find out which ones will gain the maximum support. Getting chicken parm off the menu would yield votes from the anti-chicken-slash-vegetarian-slash-easily-nauseated demographic."

More laughs. I felt my muscles loosen.

"But I'm not going to do that. You know why?"

I let the moment hang. Just like Mom would.

"Because we all know you can't trust politicians."

The room had gone quiet. I had their attention now.

"We all want a better life. We want tasty cafeteria food, more social activities, and an opportunity to do good in the world. We want a chance to get into the college of our choice. But you know what?"

Silence.

"No one can promise to give that to you, least of all a politician. You have to get it yourself."

I cocked my head to one side and raised my free hand. This was more than WWPAD. I was really hitting my stride. I was Morgan Abbott, daughter of President Sara Abbott, the first female, and youngest-elected, president in American history. I was one of a long line of women who defied the odds. My mother's campaign slogan came to my lips.

"Change starts with one person and one person only: you."

All eyes were glued on me, and for once I didn't feel weird. I felt great. Like I'd found my calling.

"I'll only make one promise to you. That you'll have a memorable senior year. And if you honor me by electing me your senior class president, we'll figure out how to make that happen together."

It was so quiet, you could hear the air conditioner hum. For one awful second, I thought I might have bored them into a coma. Then Hannah punched the air and started clapping, and a groundswell of applause rose and filled the auditorium. Soon everyone was standing. Well, except for Brittany's pink witches cabal. They looked like they were about to retch up the toadstools they'd had for lunch. I saw Brittany wrinkle her nose as if she'd stepped in dog poo.

I felt a flush creep up my cheeks. Maybe I had pulled this off after all.

I reclipped the microphone, then picked up my useless notecards and shoved them hard into the waistband of my skirt.

Big mistake.

The notecards went in and the pin I'd used to hold up my skirt popped open, stabbing me in my waist. I clutched my side, trying to hold back a wail of pain, but at the same time I noticed that I'd started peeing notecards. They dribbled to my feet, where I promptly slipped on them. As I went down, I grabbed for the podium, which left my skirt free to puddle around my ankles . . . and it did just that, while the glass of water on the podium tipped over onto the front of my blouse.

Applause turned to laughter.

"Classic Abbott!" someone yelled.

Great. Leave it to me to snatch defeat out of the jaws of victory.

Agonized, I glanced at Hannah. She stared at me in horror.

Then I remembered another rule of Mom's: When there's disaster looming, step in front of the speeding train, wave a warning, and do your best to avert a wreck. If you're lucky, you can prevent the train from derailing. Or if all else fails, at least you'll die trying.

I kicked out of my limp skirt, grateful that I'd followed through on Plan B and worn my gym shorts, leaned into the mic, and raised my voice over the hysterical laughter pinging around the auditorium.

"You've got two clear choices this election, my fellow seniors. Candy kisses and sugar-coated promises, or unpredictability. What's more fun? Vote for me, and I can guarantee one thing. Your senior year won't be boring."

I picked my skirt up off the floor and twirled it over my head. More laughs, but this time they seemed a little friendlier. Or maybe I just wanted them to seem that way.

Tears began to sting my eyes as I gritted my teeth and smiled at my classmates. For all my advance planning, I'd still managed to achieve utter humiliation. Amazing.

Brittany joined me at the front of the stage. Her sugary voice cooed in my ear while she graciously acknowledged the applause for us both: "Becoming class president will be easier than I thought. Thanks, sweetie."

If I killed her right now, do you think my mom would stay my execution?

Dad said my senior year in high school would be the time of my life. Yeah, right. I wondered if I could go on sabbatical. Check back in when I was, like, forty-seven.

I left the auditorium and ducked into the bathroom in the math hallway. When Hannah burst in I was busy drying the front of my blouse under the hand dryer.

"That was some speech," she said, giving me a quick hug. "I went to your locker and got the spare clothes you keep for emergencies. We'll fix you up in a jiff."

"Thanks, Hannah," I said, changing into my new outfit.

Hannah dug into her massive Baby Phat handbag and pulled out scarves, a tangled mass of necklaces and bangles, and her makeup brushes. Not for the first time I felt thankful my BFF wanted to major in theater makeup and costume design.

I let Hannah fuss over me while I tried my dad's tai chi mental relaxation techniques. Unfortunately, Brittany Whittaker's smirking face kept floating before me, ruining the tranquil waterfall I was trying to visualize.

"There. Looking sharp now, Morg, if I do say so myself."

I gazed at myself in the mirror. "You're a genius, Hannah."

"I know," she said without a trace of modesty.

I heaved a big sigh. "Guess I can't hide in here all day."

"Nope. We might as well head to play rehearsal. We've pretty much missed calculus."

"Calculus—crap." I was already on shaky ground with Mr. Parmentaviswala. Somehow he wasn't impressed with my solid D average.

"Well, here goes nothing." I lifted my head, exited the bathroom, and rammed right into someone blocking the way. "Denny!"

My Secret Service agent had stationed himself at the bathroom door, arms folded like a bouncer. He might as well have erected a flashing neon sign: *President's Daughter Having Nervous Breakdown Inside*.

"You okay, Morgan?" Real concern reflected in his eyes, and I swallowed the annoyed remark sparking on the tip of my tongue.

"I'm fine," I said. I knew Denny was just doing his job, but did he always have to get in the way? He was about as subtle as a chin mole with a big black hair sticking out of it.

The final bell rang and students poured into the halls. As Hannah and I made our way back to the auditorium, I got a few friendly nods and high fives.

Hannah nudged me. "See? Even all wet you can outshine Brit-Brit."

"Or maybe they're just glad I provided another freak show for them to yak about."

"No one's gonna remember this tomorrow, Morgan. You're too hard on yourself."

Before I could share my fear that my performance was already on YouTube, an arm snaked around my midsection and squeezed.

"Hey, babe!" Konner whirled me around and kissed me. "You rocked it today."

"You think so?" I felt breathless, as I always did when Konner showed me a little PDA. "Even when my skirt fell down?"

"Uh, yeah. Yeah, that was hot." He frowned.

Obviously, the puzzled wrinkle over Konner's brow meant he hadn't paid any attention to my speech, but for once I was glad.

Behind him Hannah rolled her eyes. Then she stiffened. "Uh, Morgan—"

"Hey, Davis, can't you give us some privacy?" Konner turned me toward the lockers and leaned in close. "I don't like an audience."

Over Konner's shoulder, my BFF was making a series of cryptic motions with her hands. I realized too late that it was a warning.

Chapter Three

Ms. Gibson, AOP's guidance counselor, appeared at my side. She was about twenty-five years old and looked like Angelina Jolie—not U.N. Ambassador Jolie, all friendly and helpful, but *Tomb Raider* Jolie, the one who would kick anyone's ass for fun.

"Morgan Abbott! Konner Tippington! You know the rules about inappropriate behavior in school."

Konner and I sprang apart. "Sure, Ms. Gibson," Konner said easily. "I was just congratulating Morgan on her speech."

"See to it that's all you do during school hours." Ms. Gibson's glare could cut glass. "Morgan, I need to speak with you. In. My. Office."

I shot Hannah a resigned look and waved good-bye to Konner. I glumly followed Gibson into the part of the Academy that was built during the nineteenth century. I'm talking oak paneling with portraits of stodgy old men lining the walls. We eventually arrived at the guidance counselor's office.

"Your grades stink, Morgan," she said after she settled behind her desk.

One has to appreciate Ms. Gibson's candor.

"Four Ds, an A-minus in *drama*—" Ms. Gibson barely restrained a snort of derision. "And two Cs. I've always taken you for a smart girl, Morgan, despite your poor academic record. So you tell me how you're going to be admitted to a community college, let alone a respectable university, with grades like these."

"Uh . . . I think you might have mistaken my impish charm for intelligence."

Did Gibson's lips twitch in amusement? Impossible.

Then her gaze grew steelier. "Let's put all the cards on the table. You don't get a pass here just because you're the president's daughter. Or the daughter of Sam Abbott, who single-handedly made Wi-Fi available to the entire planet at a reasonable cost. You are responsible for you. And *you* are in danger of flunking out of AOP."

My mouth went dry. This was getting serious.

"If you don't get these grades up, Morgan, you will be banned from any—and I mean *any*—extracurricular activities."

"But—"

"That means no more drama productions, including the upcoming musical, no team sports or field trips, no student council. *Nada*."

"That's *so* unfair," I said lamely. My parents' art of persuasion had clearly skipped a generation.

"If that's what it takes to get you to focus, Morgan, the school has no choice. You know we can't give you any special treatment."

I slouched in my chair. "I know."

"Change starts with one person: you."

Ouch. She *would* throw that back in my face.

Why was it I had to practically set my brain on fire studying to accomplish those Cs when Mom and Dad came out of the womb as geniuses?

"I'll do better, Ms. Gibson. I promise."

I slunk out of there as fast as I could.

Getting metaphorically walloped upside the head by Ms. Gibson was never a pleasant experience, but today's session really shook me up.

Everyone thought I had it soooo easy as First Daughter. How could I tell Ms. Gibson . . . or anyone for that matter . . . that being the president's daughter wasn't all state dinners, Easter egg hunts on the White House lawn, and trips to Africa during school breaks? The pressure of it sat on my shoulders like a lead-lined parka. Be perfect. Don't screw up. Everyone's watching you.

And when you do mess up, it's a double whammy. Not only are you an idiot, but you're the idiot who happens to be the *president's daughter*. My lousy grades reflect badly on the leader of the free world. Seriously, who can live with that kind of pressure?

I heard puffing behind me. Denny trotted at my heels. Sweat beaded around his receding hairline and he looked like he needed another macchiato. "Morgan, hey, hold up," he wheezed.

"I'm late for rehearsal, Denny."

"You haven't told me where you and the Tippington boy are going out to dinner tonight."

"Do you really need to know?"

"I need to send out an advance team to sweep the place first. You know that."

"Yeah. But the problem is, so does the entire world. We'll have the paparazzi swarming all over Augustino's before we even get there."

"Augustino's. Check."

"Denny! I said *don't* send the advance team to Augustino's. Konner and I want privacy tonight."

Denny gave me one of his looks—the sympathetic executioner. "Rules are rules, Morgan."

I was getting soooooo sick of this.

"Denny, I'm tired of being watched every minute. I can't even go to the bathroom without everyone knowing because you're practically standing outside the stall. Can I just pretend to be a normal person for one afternoon?"

A weird expression crossed his face—a combination of pity and exhaustion.

"Okay, Morgan," he said. "I'll give you some space this afternoon, as long as you don't do anything crazy."

I couldn't even muster up the grace to thank him. I needed to get moving.

Dress rehearsal had already started when I arrived at the auditorium. Finally, after three years of badgering, I convinced the drama teacher that we could handle the musical *Rent*. Well, it was my convincing paired with the fact that a school edition of the production just came out—and Konner's parents forked over the money for the royalty payment.

Up on the stage, Konner, who'd won the role of Benny the slumlord, was belting out his number in a killer three-piece suit. I paused for a moment, dazzled by his charisma and good looks. Whether on the basketball court or the stage, Konner commanded everyone's attention. Geez.

Hannah appeared at my elbow. "You survived Gibson?"

"Barely."

"Come on, I've got to get you into your costume before Escobedo throws one of his screaming hissy fits. We're behind schedule as it is."

"So, what am I wearing? Something outrageous, I hope." I'd been cast as Maureen, the bisexual performance artist. The role was as far as possible from my normal personality, which was why I loved it.

"Outrageous? It's interplanetary!" Hannah dragged me backstage. She was the production's wardrobe and makeup artist, and getting into full diva mode about it.

Ten minutes later, I was gazing at my reflection in the full-length mirror in the girls' dressing room. Hannah had poured me into skintight black PVC hot pants and a matching bustier.

"I'll tell you what's interplanetary. My boobs." I tugged at the gel cleavage enhancers Hannah had thrust down the front of the bustier, which gave my two flat pancakes a serious lift.

"You're welcome. Now shut up while I do your makeup."

Hannah applied slabs of blue eye shadow that contrasted nicely with my brown eyes, and found some purple-black lipstick for my lips. Then she swiped sparkly blush over my cheeks, which I had to admit really brought out my cheekbones.

The sour feeling left by Ms. Gibson was easing away. I loved all this: performing, getting into a role, and most of all, having a great excuse to forget about being Morgan Abbott, the president's daughter, for just a little while.

My entrance onstage caused a stir.

"Holy moley!" Jeong Nguyn said, pulling down the glasses he had to wear for the role of Mark Cohen, the Jewish mensch. "Is that you, Morgan?"

"For real." I slammed a pop 'n' lock move, which cracked everyone up.

Konner made a beeline for me. "Looking good, babe," he said, his eyes glued to my mounded breasts.

I resisted the urge to cover them with my hands. Brittany Whittaker drifted past. She'd badgered Escobedo into being his director's assistant, perfect for a control freak like her. "Making yourself a little more user-friendly, I see. How sluttastic for you, Morgan."

"Who peed in your cornflakes this morning, Brit?" Jeong remarked.

Hannah spoke up. "She's just jealous because Morgan kicked her butt at the class president speeches."

"At least I don't have to strip for votes," Brittany replied snottily.

I felt myself growing hot with anger. "Because that would be so much worse than stealing someone else's platform, *word for word*, right?"

Brittany's pink-frosted mouth thinned into a vicious line.

Konner yawned. "Yeesh. I hate it when girls fight," he said to Jeong.

"Speak for yourself," Jeong replied with an exaggerated leer. "I kinda like it."

Hannah smacked the back of his head. "Pervert. This is serious."

Brittany and I glared at each other. IT. WAS. ON.

Mr. Escobedo bounded onstage, stopping things from getting ugly. "Everyone take five," he shouted, even though we were standing right next to him. "We've got a problem with the lighting that needs to be fixed before we can continue rehearsal. Don't wander away!"

Immediately, everyone began wandering away.

Konner whispered in my ear. "You look amazing, Morgan."

Tingles shot through me. "So do you," I murmured, allowing my eyes to slide appreciatively over his six-foot-two-inch frame lovingly tucked inside that smokin' three-piece suit.

"Come on." He tugged my hand and I willingly followed him into the prop room, which was filled with a jumble of rejects from past drama productions.

I ignored the smell of mold and plastic, then forgot about it altogether when Konner drew me close. "Wow, Morgan," he said, giving my boobs another long look before lowering his face to mine. "Wow."

Konner, it must be said, kissed like the babe-magnet he was. I tried not to think about all the girls he'd practiced on before me, but still, I appreciated their unspoken service.

That is, until I felt his breathing change.

His hands, which had been running up and down my back, now wandered to the front of my bustier, and the lack of oxygen from his increasingly hard kisses made my head spin.

I broke the kiss. "Konner. Wait—"

"Come on, babe." He started gnawing on the side of my neck. His teeth felt sharp and his hand squeezed my gel enhancers.

"Konner! I said stop—"

Suddenly the door of the prop room burst open.

"Freeze right there! Step away from the president's daughter."

In horror, I looked over Konner's shoulder and saw not only Denny, my Secret Service agent, but a *team* of agents.

He called in the perimeter detail? Unbelievable.

And behind them, Brittany and AOP's entire drama class craned to get a gander at us.

The only thing missing from this freak show was the popcorn.

Chapter Four

"Denny! What's going on?" I yelled.

By now Konner had been wrestled away from me by a couple of agents and was being frisked. The expression on Konner's face was something I wouldn't soon forget: one part humiliation and ten parts pissed off. "Morgan! Call off your goons, will ya?"

"Denny!"

"He's clean," said one of the agents who was keeping a tight grip on Konner's shoulder.

"Of course he's clean; he's my boyfriend," I told him angrily.

"Probably not after this," I heard Brittany say snidely. The agents were communicating with devices implanted in their earpieces. "Yep, false alarm—*again*," I heard one say.

Mr. Escobedo quickly herded the drama class away from the prop room, but that didn't spare me the sight of Brittany's satisfied smirk.

I rounded on Denny. "I demand an explanation."

Denny pocketed his portable GPS tracking device—the one where I was the little red flashing dot. "Simple, Morgan. Through window surveillance, one of the perimeter team agents saw you being shoved into a closet. When he called me for clarification, I had to tell him I didn't know where you were."

"Does that mean barging in, guns blazing?"

"You broke The Bubble, Morgan. I had to act."

The Bubble. Agent-speak for the zone of protection around the president and her family.

"You told me you wouldn't do anything stupid," Denny continued.

"Correction. I told you I wouldn't do anything crazy." Because stupid's something I've got a lock on.

As furious as I was, I really couldn't blame Denny for doing his job. To be honest, beneath my shock and embarrassment, I was a little relieved. Konner and his wandering hands had gone too far, and I had a real moment of doubt that I could get him to back off.

Speaking of Konner—

"Hey, bro. Could you let me go?" Konner twitched under the perimeter agent's special restraining grip. "Morgan?"

Denny nodded to the agent, who gave Konner a don't-give-me-any-b.s. scowl before releasing him.

"Watch the threads, dude." Konner smoothed the lapels of his suit before heading to the auditorium door.

"Text me later," I called after him.

"Yeah, whatever," he replied sullenly.

A second perimeter agent approached Denny. "POTUS is in the hold," he told him.

POTUS. President of the United States. "The hold" was the Oval Office.

"Your mom is waiting for us," Denny said. I had to admit, he kept a pretty good game face on, considering he was about to get reamed for this. "Get the motorcade ready and let's roll."

I glanced down at my skimpy costume. My gel enhancers had gone wonky due to Konner's roving hands. "Can you at least let me change and talk to Mr. Escobado before you bring the Baby Beast limo around?"

"No. Mr. Escobado has been informed." Denny had kicked into full-on official Secret Service mode. There'd be no more negotiating with him today. Or until my mom's term in office expired, probably.

I sighed. I wasn't real eager to see my mom right now. She wasn't going to be happy about being interrupted over another one of "Morgan's little episodes."

Man, how I wished I could stay out of trouble for just one day.

A delegation of Japanese dignitaries was giving a press conference in front of the North Portico, my usual entry into the White House. Media presence would be intense, so Denny had the team drive me to the West Wing entry, which I usually avoided because it swarmed with Cabinet appointees, D.C. powerbrokers, diplomats, an army of staff members, and the press. From there, I'd meet my mom in the Oval Office.

As I got out of the motorcade, I clutched the trench coat that I'd pilfered from the prop room to my throat. Underneath the coat, my PVC hot pants chafed and crept up into all the wrong places. I'd managed to remove most of Hannah's pancake makeup in the limo, but now my face somehow felt both naked and smudgy. I kept my head down and walked quickly toward the door, flanked by agents.

I scooted by one of the marines guarding the entry and nearly bumped into a massive vase full of white lilies—Mom's favorite flower—sitting smack-dab on the Madison-era hall table. My nose began its telltale tingle and I sneezed. Gah, I'm beyond allergic to lilies. Mom reminded her staff about it, but fawning diplomats kept sending them anyway. I sneezed again.

Julia, one of Mom's deputy chiefs of staff, was power walking by, arms loaded with files. "Bless you, Madam President," she said cheerily.

I raised my head, sniffling like a spaniel puppy. Julia checked her step and flushed. "Goodness, Morgan! I took you for your mother. Wow, you're the spitting image of her. When did you get to be such a big girl?"

Appalled, I stared at her. I didn't know which insulted me more: the fact that she thought I was a *big* girl now, or that I looked so much like my mother. Despite being in her early forties and blessed with preternaturally youthful skin, Mom didn't believe in chasing trends or wearing shoes with anything resembling a heel. I guess the unlimited power of the presidency drains a person of all sense of style. The media said her style was classic; I thought her style was just plain old-fashioned. And *that* was what I looked like?

Reluctantly, I conceded that it wasn't Julia's fault that she'd misidentified me. I *was* wrapped in the trench coat, plus with my hair being a bit longer than normal and without its usual streaks of neon hair color, I had somehow ended up with something approaching my mom's hairstyle. Arg!

Julia's eyes swept over my smudged lips and raccoon eyes. "Maybe I should call my optometrist and make an appointment," she muttered.

Denny asserted himself. He was clearly ready to get this over with. "Morgan's expected in the Oval Office," he told Julia. She got the hint and resumed her power-walk down the corridor.

Padma, Mom's private secretary, did a double take when I entered her office in the executive suite, but she recovered quickly. "Go right in. The president had to step away for an emergency meeting, but she won't be long." Padma'd gotten used to my unique fashion sense and flare for total catastrophe over the year she'd been Mom's gatekeeper, and she smiled at me sympathetically.

"Thanks, Pads. Got any toffees left? I'm starved."

"You know where to find them. Help yourself." Padma kept a stash of candy imported from her hometown of Mumbai on a shelf next to her desk. I took a couple. These toffees rocked. The boiled chocolate limes—not so much.

Denny checked the peephole in the door leading to the Oval Office before opening it. The detail ushered me in, and I flopped onto one of the plush couches flanking the presidential seal woven into the gold-and-blue area rug.

Denny and team stationed themselves at the windows and doors. I popped a toffee and studied the portrait of George Washington hanging over the fireplace. At the opposite end of the room, neat stacks of papers loaded the famous Resolute Desk. When Mom sat behind it, she'd have to stare at ol' George smiling tightly down at her day in and day out. Someone had placed a bowl of pale pink peonies on the Federalist coffee table instead of lilies, thank god. Afternoon sun burnished the creams, golds, and blues of the decor, muting the colors even further. The Oval Office was cool, what with all the monumental history that had gone down in here, but something about it bored me. Bad feng shui, I guess. A pop of red or purple would do wonders. Maybe a lava lamp or something, just to bring it into the last century.

The door leading to the Cabinet Room opened and the agents sprang to attention. Mom walked in.

"Madam President," Denny said deferentially. The tension coming from the detail was palpable.

I popped another toffee in my mouth.

"I'd like to speak to my daughter alone, please." My mom never raised her voice above a pleasant tone, but that didn't fool anyone.

The room cleared in three seconds flat.

Chapter Five

There was a long moment of silence. Mom perched on the edge of the Resolute Desk and toyed with a plaque, hand-carved by a famous Gullah Island artist, which bore her motto: The People Come First. The silence grew. But that was the point. I'd seen Mom make renegade senators sweat until they needed to change their shirts. They'd blurt out something stupid just to fill the silence. Then Mom would pounce.

It wouldn't work with me. No way I would crack.

At last Mom smoothed down an unnoticeably errant strand of mahogany hair in her classic bob. "I suppose you know why I asked you to come to the office."

"Nope."

"A level-three security threat, Morgan. Your father and I were scared witless when they couldn't find you."

"Denny overreacted," I said defensively. "He just doesn't get it. He shouldn't have brought in the perimeter detail."

"We're not talking about Denny right now, Morgan. We're talking about you."

"Yeah, but when we talk about me, I always end up in trouble."

Mom ignored my retort. "Honestly, I don't know what's gotten into you these days."

"Oh, I don't know, maybe my mom became president."

Mom's cocoa-colored eyes widened. "You can't blame me for everything. You need to focus, Morgan. You'll never reach your goals if you don't."

"I'm not you, Mom. I don't need, or want for that matter, to plot everything out months in advance. Stop trying to fit me into your mold."

The counterattack didn't work this time.

"Ms. Gibson called and talked to your father."

Uh-oh.

"Your grades are appalling. Four Ds? I had no idea. Are you getting mixed up with the wrong crowd?"

"No, Mom! Relax. You try to study calculus or organic chemistry knowing that a Secret Service agent is looking over your shoulder. And the perimeter detail makes AOP feel like a jail, not a school."

Mom flushed. "The security is for your safety, Morgan. You know that."

"But it's ruining my life!"

"We're getting off track." Mom took a calming breath and the color on her cheeks mellowed a bit. Her eyes became chips of ice.

Here it comes.

"If you don't get your grades up by the end of the semester, you'll be grounded until you do."

OMG, that might be forever. "Mom!" I wailed.

"And I don't want to receive any more disturbing reports about you and that boyfriend of yours . . . in a *broom* closet."

"Prop room," I muttered.

"Does that make it better? That sort of behavior won't be tolerated. I'm not even going to get into the embarrassment you caused to both yourself and the office of the presidency this time. Like it or not, we're supposed to be role models for the nation."

I didn't have a response for that, so I retreated into sulky silence. Mom plowed on with her lecture on image-shaping and public perception, and I listened with half an ear. I really hated how Mom talked to people in bullet points now—her own family included. I missed the cozy chats we used to have where we'd giggle and eat ice cream. Back when I thought I could tell her anything. But now . . . I don't know. A barrier had sprung up between us when she became president. There was no way I could imagine talking to the nation's commander in chief about Konner or how he was moving way too fast for me. I couldn't tell her that I didn't want to lose my boyfriend, but I wasn't sure I could handle him, either.

Mom's voice interrupted my thoughts. "Well? Any rebuttal?"

"I didn't run for office."

"What's that supposed to mean?"

"It means that I never wanted all this attention, Mom. It's not fair that I have to think everything through a bajillion times before I take action because I have to worry that the media or the nation or the freaking *president of the United States* will judge me. Why does *your* job have to ruin *my* life?"

Mom flinched. I couldn't believe it—her eyes were welling up with tears. I felt my own eyes start stinging.

A chirping noise from the intercom on her desk snapped us both out of it. Mom broke eye contact first and hit the com button. Padma's voice warbled out. "He's here now, Sara."

"Thanks. Give me one minute, then send him in." Mom sighed and stood up. "As much as I want to continue this conversation with you, I honestly don't have time."

"Do you ever?"

She ignored my snarky retort. "I'm heading to Africa on Friday for a series of crucial meetings. But when I get back, we'll have a good long discussion. Just you and me."

I shrugged. I've heard that line too many times to take it seriously anymore.

My trench coat, which I'd loosened because the plastic hot pants and tight bustier were making me sweat like a pig, slipped off my shoulder.

Mom's head snapped around. "Morgan, what on earth are you wearing?"

I looked down. My gel enhancers had forced one boob higher than the other. "Oh, it's a—"

The office side door swung open.

"Max Jackson to see . . . you." Padma's voice faltered when she caught sight of me on the couch.

Behind her, a young man with short-cropped curly brown hair entered. I cinched the coat tight again, but it was too late. The dude had gotten an eyeful.

He paused only a fraction of a heartbeat before he beelined for my mom, hand outstretched. "President Abbott. This is an honor."

Mom gripped his hand firmly and gave him one of her legendary smiles, the one that could power small cities in China with its megawatt charm. "May I introduce my daughter, Morgan? Morgan, Max Jackson."

"Hi." This Jackson guy was probably a congressional intern from some underprivileged high school or a national spelling-bee winner or something.

"Nice to meet you, Morgan," he said.

His stance was pretty solid for a high school kid, though. He didn't sweat or fidget in the presence of the president.

Mom was watching us carefully. "Max is going to be the head agent on your Secret Service detail."

What!? Was she kidding? The guy looked like he should be asking me if I wanted fries with my burger. Then I noticed the small round Secret Service pin on the lapel of his gray suit—the one that held a tracking device for all agents.

She wasn't kidding.

"Are you sure he's old enough to drive?" I blurted.

Agent Jackson's blue eyes regarded me without a smidge of irritation. "I get that all the time," he said to my mom, who chuckled.

Okay, I really hated the way he just made me feel like a snotty brat. Even if I *was* being one. I didn't like the way this was going.

"What about Denny?" I asked, trying my best to keep any sign of desperation out of my voice.

"Denny's paid his dues, Morgan, don't you think? Special Agent Jackson has been specially trained for this detail. Your father and I felt that a change in your security team was due, and after today's fiasco, I'm convinced more than ever that Agent Jackson will be the right person to shadow you."

I couldn't believe this. "But he's my age."

"That's the point," Mom said.

"Actually, I'm twenty," Max interjected.

"That's only two years older than I am."

I glared at him. I don't know why, but something about this guy really set my teeth on edge. "What if a terrorist tries to kidnap me? What's he going to do, chase after him with a skateboard?"

"Agent Jackson is fully trained, Morgan. I have every confidence that as the inside agent on your detail, he'll act appropriately to any threat. He's young, yes, but brilliant. I'm not about to discount an able agent because of youth."

I remembered that Mom had to fight a lot of age prejudice early in her term, and she wasn't going to back down on the matter.

"If it will ease your mind further, Agent Jackson's part of a classified program within the National Security Agency, which has put him through the rigors of security training for the presidency. That's all I can tell you."

I recognized the tone in Mom's voice. It was a done deal, and nothing I could say would change her mind.

Frustration, anger, and helplessness welled up in my chest like a big ball of fire. I hate-hate-hated how decisions affecting *my life* were made without consulting me first. "Why can't everyone leave me alone?" I cried. "I just want to be a normal person for once."

Mom wasn't having it. "That's not possible for us anymore."

I turned to make a dramatic exit but as I did so bumped into the bowl of peonies. Water spilled all over the rug in a classic Morgan Abbott moment. Embarrassment swamped me.

Mom put her hands on her hips. "All right, missy. That's it. You're grounded for the rest of the night."

"But I didn't mean . . ."

"The time for excuses is over. Maybe an evening hitting the books will put things in perspective for you."

"But I'm going out with Konner tonight."

"You'll have to cancel your plans."

"You may be the ruler of the free world, but you can't run *my life*!" I pushed Agent Jackson out of the way and stormed out.

Chapter Six

I rushed out of the Oval Office, down the center hall that
connected the West Wing to the East Wing, and shoved my
way through a tour group with necks craned upward while one
of the White House docents droned on about the Truman-era
vaulted ceilings. I pounded up the back stairs to the third-floor
residence, anger and frustration boiling in my gut. God, this day
had gone from bad to worse.

I headed to my bedroom, but when I reached the door, I
realized that Boy Scout/Secret Service agent Max Jackson had
kept pace right behind me.

I stormed into my room and slammed the door in his face.

That felt pretty good for about one second. Then it felt like
one of a million horrible things I'd done wrong today.

Tears threatened, but I held them back. I hadn't been a
crybaby in the past, and I wasn't about to start now.

After a long moment, I threw myself on the bed and dug

my cell phone out of the pocket of the trench coat. I dialed Konner's number. Even though I was dreading delivering the bad news about our canceled plans, I was anxious to hear his voice. Maybe I could smooth things over about what went down in the prop room.

"Hey, babe, what's up?" Konner's voice sounded normal, if a little distant.

I bit my lip. This was gonna suck. "Hey. I have to cancel our dinner date tonight."

"What'd you say?" The sounds of body blows and explosions rang out in the background. Konner made no excuses for his Ninja Mêlée game addiction. I'd learned to live with it.

"I said, I have to cancel dinner tonight. Mom had a fit about . . . you know, what happened at rehearsal. I'm grounded."

"Bummer. Oh, man, I nailed him! A two-hundred-point kill."

"Are you still mad at me?"

"Mad at you?"

"About us . . . in the prop room . . . I'm just not ready. . . . I hope you understand. . . ."

"Yeah, I get it, babe. But it was sorta your fault."

"*My* fault?"

"You don't know your power over me. You looked smokin' in that outfit, I lost it."

43

I blushed. I loved how Konner made me feel like the hottest girl alive.

More lasers, explosions. Sounds of screaming ninjas being wasted. "Awesome!" Konner yelled. "I'm ripping up this level."

I frowned. "Well, I wouldn't want to keep you from accomplishing anything as important as getting to level five in a video game." I didn't bother to hide the sarcasm.

"Thanks, babe."

I flipped the phone shut. I still felt crappy.

My stomach growled. Nerves from my class-president speech had prevented me from wolfing down my usual lunch. I checked my purple clock radio with the googly-eye antennas. Three hours before our official dinnertime. My life is so scheduled. I deserved a snack before I hit the books to study for tomorrow's psych test.

Thankfully, Agent Jackson wasn't lurking in the halls of the family wing when I emerged wearing a T-shirt, shorts, and flip-flops. Like all agents, it looked like he was going to leave me alone once I was inside the protective zone of the White House's third floor. Still, surveillance cameras and personalized tracking devices made it virtually impossible to escape the feeling of being watched.

I hated it.

The delicious smell of braised meat and caramelized onions hit me when I entered the White House kitchen. My appetite exploded.

"Hey, Nigel!" I waved to the White House's executive chef, who was bending over a pasta machine. "Need some help?"

A big smile split Nigel Bellingham's face, which was the color of cooked lobster under his chef's toque hat. "Of course, luvvie. I can always use a spare set of hands."

Sous chefs and sauciers moved in smooth choreography over the eight-burner stove. Flames leaped and meats sizzled. Mom and Dad were hosting a dinner of congressional delegates that night and the kitchen was in full swing.

I scrabbled in the cookie jar for a handful of Nigel's famous white-chocolate gingersnaps. Brittany's snarky remark about my fat ass floated through my mind. I shrugged. She could kiss my fat ass for all I cared.

I wolfed down a cookie. "Put me to work, Nigel. I need some distraction."

"Everything okay, Morgan, luv?"

Nigel could always be counted on to listen. I opened my mouth to tell him about my bad day when I caught sight of a figure in a gray suit and tie hovering over by the coolers, trying to stay out of the way of the busy kitchen staff.

"What's he doing in here?" I asked Nigel.

"Who? Agent Jackson? He's new on the detail, he tells me. Cracking chap, too. He helped Maria lug in a crate of oranges without being asked. That boy has manners."

I didn't want to hear about Agent Jackson's manners or see

the guy more than I absolutely had to. I turned my back on him. "Could we get rid of him? I think I'm allergic to him."

"Sorry, luv. Rules are rules."

I snorted. "Rules are made to be broken."

Nigel chuckled. "I'm sure she didn't mean that, Agent Jackson."

I spun around. The guy was right behind me! Ugh! The expression on his face was one I recognized from every Secret Service agent ever assigned to me. Calculation, with a hint of tension.

I felt guilty for a moment about my earlier allergic comment, not that he'd care—I was just a job. I quickly turned and began spooning mushroom mascarpone filling into fresh ravioli squares while Nigel crimped the sides and listened to me blab about Brittany stealing my election platform and the horrible session with Ms. Gibson. The debacle in the prop room with Konner I kept to myself, especially with Agent Jackson hovering around. Some things were too embarrassing to talk about. Everyone probably already knew anyway. The First Daughter has no secrets.

Every time I glanced up, I found Agent Jackson standing with hands folded before him, feet planted in the solid stance that they must teach all agents at Secret Service boot camp. Every so often, he would mutter into the wireless mic clipped to the lapel of his suit.

"Copy that," he said at one point. "Tornado's in the kitchen."

Tornado. My Secret Service code name.

"It's under control. She seems calmer now. Bellingham's keeping her busy and—"

Calmer? Busy? Was I three years old now?

I was so sick of every action I took being dissected by the Secret Service, the media, the office of protocol, or Brittany Whittaker, like I was a lab experiment or a mutant life-form.

Agent Jackson was scribbling something in a pocket notepad when I murmured "See ya around" to Nigel and ducked out of the kitchen. I'd had enough of surveillance and com reports on my actions for one day.

I slipped off my flip-flops and booked as fast as I could across the center hall. My bare feet slapped on the marble floor as I skidded into the Map Room. The White House cleaning staff had recently rearranged the Victorian furnishings to better display the collection of historic maps, so I miscalculated the Chippendale table's new location and hit my bare toe against the wooden leg. Biting back the pain, I steadied the wobbly Chinese vase—certain to be a priceless artifact—and hopped across the thick Persian rug to the door connecting to the Diplomatic Room.

I opened the door. Agent Jackson stood on the other side.

"Going somewhere?" he asked.

Shoooooooot.

I tried to stay cool. Hard to do when your toe kills and you're out of breath. "Where I'm going is none of your business."

"Uh, yes, it is. Starting today, where you go is my entire world."

I edged into the Diplomatic Room. The oval-shaped room happened to be my favorite because it showed some style: A crystal chandelier threw sparks against the walls, which sported a landscape panorama of nineteenth-century Americana. The handwoven blue-and-yellow rug bore emblems from each of the fifty states. Best of all, one of the panels concealed a secret passage that led directly to the South Lawn. If I could just get to the panel . . .

"Do you mind?" I said coolly, inching toward the panel. "You're in my personal space."

"I apologize." Agent Jackson took a step back before deliberately moving in front of the secret passage panel and planting himself in front of it.

Damn it!

Nonchalantly I strolled to the opposite end of the room. Two could play this game. I opened the door that led to the China Room, and before Agent Jackson could move, I slammed it shut behind me. This door had a lock on it. Ha-ha.

I threw the lock home and darted across the room, which was decorated in royal red and white to better display the massive collection of china plates from the previous presidencies. I waved at the portrait of Mrs. Calvin Coolidge, who smiled approvingly down at me. I always liked Mrs. Coolidge, because she showed mad 1920s flapper style.

I opened the connecting door to the Vermeil Room, a space that had to remain a boring shade of yellow and green to complement the White House's collection of gold-plated silver. Stodgy Duncan Phyfe—furniture that nobody seemed to like— was warehoused here.

Agent Jackson stood, arms folded, under a portrait of Nancy Reagan. "Are we going to play this game all afternoon, Morgan?" he asked wearily.

I ground my teeth over a curse word.

"Why don't you make this easy on both of us and stop trying to run away?" he continued.

"I'm not running away, I'm trying to get a little privacy. How would you feel if you had agents tripping on your heels all day long?"

"You know as well as I do that the second you leave the secured confines of the third floor, an agent has to shadow you at all times to maintain your bubble of security."

"God!" I couldn't help yelling. "I'm in The Bubble twenty-four-seven. The Bubble is suffocating me. I'm sick of it!"

"The president thought you might feel that way after what happened today with the perimeter detail. That's why she wanted me to tail you this afternoon—so you wouldn't breach security."

I wanted to die. Right after I killed my mom for being a blabbermouth. It could be a double state funeral. "Mom told you about what happened at rehearsal today?"

"Of course not."

The agent's baby face gave no hint of what he was thinking. The perfect Secret Service agent.

"I read the report."

No. Nononononooooooo. Somewhere in the bowels of the Secret Service agency, people were reading a report on the X-rated misadventures of Morgan Abbott.

I took a deep breath. "Okay. You win. I'll head upstairs to the family wing."

"Excellent."

"You can take a coffee break or something."

"How about I go with you instead?"

"I'm not going to run away."

"I appreciate that. And maybe you can appreciate that I'm only doing my job. Think of our mutual understanding as reaching detente."

"Like Nixon and China?" I answered scathingly. "Another landmark negotiation treaty?"

"Exactly." He smiled a little in spite of himself.

I sighed. "If I'm stuck with you for the rest of the day, I'm gonna put you to work."

A flash of alarm cracked through his impassive expression. It was only for a second but it was satisfying to watch.

I turned the screw. "You can help me study for my psych test."

"Bring it," he said with a touch of relief. "I have a degree in psychology. And criminology."

"Really?"

"And political science."

"Three bachelor's degrees? How's that possible? You're only twenty, right?"

To my surprise, a flush crept across his face. "I'm, uh, able to process information at a rapid rate. Numbers, equations. Situations. Something I was born with."

"A genius, huh?"

He brushed off my remark. "Nah. I'm just able to focus." Ouch. Lack of focus was definitely my problem, according to Ms. Gibson.

I didn't want to admit it, but Max Jackson impressed me. My new Secret Service agent was Einstein with a gun.

We headed upstairs to the family wing and I grabbed the books in my room while Max waited for me in the Clinton-era kitchenette at the end of the hall. The table there was big enough to spread out all my books. Per my request, the kitchen sent up two orders of Nigel's killer cowboy burgers with onion rings instead of the healthy grilled fish scheduled for tonight's dinner. Max then drilled me on Erikson's eight stages of psychosocial development, but my brain felt like it couldn't get past the second stage.

"That's it," he said when I was able to successfully diagram the psychosocial stages on a chart. "I think you've got it nailed."

"Really?" I felt a level of confidence for an upcoming test that I hadn't experienced in a long time.

Max pushed back from the table.

"Where are you going?" I asked. "Do you want another soda? Or I could have the kitchen send up a batch of Nigel's cookies?"

"No, thanks. I need to do some paperwork before I punch out."

I glanced at the clock. It was nearly ten p.m. Mom and Dad would be coming up from the congressional dinner pretty soon.

"The night detail is already in place," Max went on. "I've got to be back here bright and early to take you to school."

Now I felt bad, because agent rotation usually occurred at seven p.m. Max stayed an extra three hours past his shift to help me study.

"You've been a big help." I gave Max a sincere smile. It was nice having a Secret Service agent who acted nearly human.

To my surprise, Max scowled. "I'll be waiting downstairs

with the Baby Beast at eight sharp. I'd appreciate it if you weren't late tomorrow."

Just like that, the friendly agent had turned back into a Secret Service robot. "Who told you I was late in the mornings?"

"It's legendary in the agency."

I slammed my psych book shut. "Well, don't worry. I'll be on time. I'll even be early, because I want to pick up my boyfriend on the way." That last bit came to me out of the blue, but the more I thought about it, the more I liked the idea.

Max refused to be baited. "Great. See you tomorrow."

"Excellent. See ya."

I waited until he left the room. Then I pulled out my cell phone and flipped it open. I needed to text Konner to tell him I'd be picking him up tomorrow and then I needed to call Hannah—we had to strategize about tomorrow's election. Oh, and she *had* to hear about my new Secret Agent Man.

Chapter Seven

Morning came too soon, as usual, but the thought of Agent Jackson telling the other agents that Tornado was late again made me get up after hitting the snooze button only twice. I ran a comb through my hair, pulled on my favorite GUMBY RULES THE WORLD T-shirt and jeans, and texted Konner a reminder that I'd swing by in the Baby Beast to pick him up on the way to school.

Agent Jackson, wearing his gray suit and probably a government-issue tie, nodded a greeting as I got in the car. He made no comment when I told the driver to stop by Konner's house in a historic area of Georgetown. Obviously he was all business now. I settled back into the leather seats of the Baby Beast and focused on the specially reinforced smoked-glass windows while we fought the traffic on Pennsylvania Avenue.

As soon as we pulled up to the expensive line of brick row houses, Konner bounded down the steps from his front door. He loved driving in the motorcade almost as much as I hated it.

"Hey, babe!" Konner smacked a kiss on my temple. "You look hot today."

"Thanks." I glanced at Max, but Special Agent Jackson kept his attention squarely on the GPS unit in his hand.

"Can we turn on the TV?" Konner asked. "I wanna catch the score from the Redskins game."

"Sure."

Konner hit a button on the panel, and a mini TV screen lowered from the limo's roof. ESPN *Sportsnet* blared into the car as we headed north toward the Chevy Chase district, where long ago, the first headmaster of Academy of the Potomac bought the land that would become the site of the school. Little did he know that one day, that land would become the most coveted patch of real estate on the Maryland border.

Konner slung his arm around my shoulders and pulled me close. "Hey, I've got an idea," he said. "How about we try going out again tonight? You can have the White House social secretary hook us up with reservations to Mikyasa. I hear it's the hottest sushi bar in the Metro area."

"That'd be great," I said happily. "Agent Jackson can send an advance detail this afternoon to sweep the place. Can't you, Agent Jackson?"

Max nodded. He was studying Konner with a face clean of

expression. Konner didn't notice. But I sure did.

"Let's pull over here," I said when we were about a block away from the Academy.

Konner rolled his eyes. "C'mon, Morgan, what's the big deal about driving through the gate?"

"You know I don't like pulling up in a chauffeured limo. I already get enough negative attention as it is. Besides, it's really nice out. Let's get some fresh air before we're cooped up inside all day."

A sound of annoyance rumbled in Konner's throat, but he swallowed it down. "Hey, bro, could you get the door?" he said to Agent Jackson.

"Konner!" I exclaimed.

Max's face never changed. "Maybe now would be a good time to explain some ground rules to you, Konner. I'm here to protect the daughter of the president of the United States. Period. I don't open car doors, I don't carry backpacks, and I don't get called 'bro.' Are we clear?"

"Sure, Jackson. Sure." Konner slid out of the limo. I quickly followed. "Man, the new guy is touchy," Konner whispered.

I cringed and hoped Max didn't hear that.

Konner and I made a date to eat lunch together before he took off to meet his posse. Hannah was waiting for me on the front steps like always. Last-minute campaigning for class president would be hot and heavy today, and Mom taught me that you needed to hustle for every single vote. Hannah carried a bag of buttons we'd made last weekend. I thought her leather fringe vest loaded with VOTE FOR MORGAN buttons was sweet.

She gave Max, who was standing just behind me, the once-over. "So this is the new man in black?" she murmured admiringly.

"Huh? Oh yeah, that's Agent Jackson."

"He looks pretty fine for a government-issued boy. Why didn't you tell me?" Hannah indiscreetly checked Max out over the rim of her sunglasses.

"Is he? I didn't notice."

Hannah laughed. "How could you not notice a smokin' bod like that?"

"Don't get too excited. He's not into fun." I glanced over my shoulder to see if Agent Jackson heard the last bit. But his face revealed nothing. "Come on, maybe we can hand out some more buttons before first period."

Hannah and I headed through the school's main hallway.

"Hi, Stacy!" I called cheerily to a girl trying to shove a massive backpack into her locker. "How did the algebra test go yesterday?"

Stacy paused midshove. Then she erupted into a fit of giggling.

Weird.

"Hey, Carl." I gave a head-nod to AOP's star freestyle

swimmer cruising by in a sweatsuit. "Practice go okay?"

Carl halted. Then he turned beet red and hurried past Hannah and me.

That's when I noticed students clustered in knots, giggling and whispering.

I turned to Hannah. "What's going on?"

Hannah looked confused, too. "I'll find out."

The bell rang. So much for last-minute campaigning.

I stepped into homeroom and the room immediately fell silent. Then I noticed Max had followed me inside.

"You don't have to attend the class," I snapped. "Denny always waited out in the hall."

"I need to keep you in visual contact at all times," he answered.

"If kidnappers somehow breached school property with the perimeter detail on the scene, they'd be bored into submission by Mr. Franken before they could reach me," I whispered. "Honestly, I'm super safe. Plus you're making everyone nervous. It's hard to concentrate with a Secret Service agent breathing down your neck."

Max's eyes shifted around the room. The entire class had fallen silent, watching him. Even Mr. Franken.

"Okay. You win this one, Morgan. I'll be right outside."

Round one to Morgan Abbott.

It wasn't until the end of second period, as we walked to our chemistry class, that Hannah was able to dial me in to what was going on with my bizarre reception at AOP this morning. She waited until Max had gone ahead to sweep the next classroom.

"Check this out," Hannah said grimly. She handed me a copy of the *D.C. Gadfly*, a tabloid gossip rag that regularly took shots at Mom and her administration.

"Oh god," I breathed.

Splashed on the cover in a grainy photo that looked like it was taken with a cell phone was me in my *Rent* costume. My boobs looked huge popping out of the bustier, and in the crazy theater makeup I could double as a pop star right before entering rehab. The headline read: PRESIDENT ABBOTT'S WILD CHILD—FALLING GRADES, TRASHY FASHION: CAN MORGAN ABBOTT BE SAVED?

And I thought yesterday was about as bad as a day could get.

Wrong again.

Chapter Eight

How could this have happened?

My mind raced. Only a few people even saw me wearing the *Rent* costume before the dress rehearsal was canceled: Konner, Jeong, Hannah, Brit—

Brittany Whittaker.

Hannah tried to take the paper out of my hands, but I snatched it back and opened to the center spread.

> **Administrators for the tony Academy of the Potomac have been increasingly concerned about the bizarre behavior of President Abbott's eighteen-year-old daughter. "She's been called to the office, like, seventeen times over the semester," says a pal. "Any other student would have been expelled by now. But since Morgan is an Abbott, she gets**

away with everything. She's stuck-up, too. Everyone's really sick of it."

Hannah eased the paper out of my numb hands. "C'mon, Morgan, don't read any more of this trash. Let's go to class."

I couldn't find the words to answer Hannah. I was in shock that someone would think I was stuck-up. Also, I'd never had to deal with negative publicity before. As soon as she was sworn into office, Mom issued an edict to the press corps to leave me alone so I could try to have as normal a life as possible. Amazingly, the press respected the request. Until now.

With Hannah's protective arm around me, I walked to chemistry class, head down. I couldn't bear the staring. Titters and whispers followed me in the halls. Could things get any worse?

Uh, yeah.

Just before we reached the classroom door, Hannah paused. "Morgan, hold up a sec."

I looked up to see Max ripping down a blown-up image of my front-page exposé taped to the door. I caught a glimpse of hand-drawn arrows pointing to my boobs with the words *Hail to the Jugs*.

Max crumpled the paper with one hand while he spoke into his com. I caught the words *investigation, track down instigators, constitute harassment of the First Family . . .*

"Don't worry," he said to me. "We'll find the perpetrators and put an end to this."

"It's okay," I told him. "Just drop it. You'll only make things worse. Mom says ignoring bad press makes it go away in three days. If we make a huge stink, the story lives on. It's no big deal."

I thought I glimpsed admiration flitting across Max's face before the iron curtain of Secret Service training came down.

"Plus, there are ways of getting back at people," Hannah said. "Unofficially, of course."

Did I mention how much I loved Hannah?

The bell rang, and Hannah and I went into the chemistry lab. Max stayed outside without me having to remind him. For the next forty-five minutes I stared unseeingly at my chem textbook. The *Gadfly* article insinuated that I used my mom's position to get special treatment. That was so untrue. I'd bent over backward *not* to get preferential treatment at school. And being called stuck-up really hurt. I thought I'd done a pretty good job of being friendly to everyone and anyone who'd let me. I hated stuck-up snobs like Brittany Whittaker. Though I couldn't prove it, I was sure Brittany was behind this.

Zombielike, I plugged away through the rest of the morning and even managed to cast my class-president vote. By lunchtime, my balance returned. Or at least I got better at hiding my humiliation. Even though I had little appetite, I met up with Konner in the cafeteria, as promised.

I toyed with a limp fishwich and fries. "Konner, I'm really sorry if that awful picture of me in the paper embarrassed you."

Konner, who'd just inhaled half a double-patty burger, swallowed. "Embarrassed? I think it rules! You're on the front page of the *Gadfly*, and you look hot. I've got the page pinned up in my locker."

"But Konner—"

"It's gonna be the top download on Celebricity.com for sure, Morgan. Probably for weeks, too. Man, you can't buy publicity like that."

Horror burst over me. "Oh my god, really? Weeks?"

"Hell, yeah! Dudes around the world will be lovin' all over your killer curves." He chomped another bite of his burger.

Reeling, I pushed away my tray. This was way worse than I expected.

I caught sight of Max standing nearby. He rolled his eyes at Konner's words. It ticked me off that someone like Max would judge my boyfriend. Sure, Konner wasn't the most sensitive guy on the planet, but Max didn't get how lucky I was to have the hottest, most popular guy at AOP as my boyfriend.

I snuggled closer to Konner, who grunted through his burger and put his arm around my shoulders. Konner swallowed. "Hey, babe," he whispered, nuzzling my neck. "Wanna sneak off to the prop room again?"

I drew away a little. "After yesterday's fiasco? No way!"

"C'mon. I know you're upset about the newspaper. But I'll get your mind off your problems."

Konner raised his brow and smiled in a way that could curl the toes of nuns.

"I don't think it's a good idea," I said, mind racing. I knew what he was asking for. "My new Secret Service agent is . . . uh, more by the book than Denny was."

"Oh yeah. That Jackson dude." Konner shot Max a cold glare that had been known to freeze lesser mortals dead, like freshmen who didn't know better than to cut in front of Konner in the lunchroom line. "Well, I hope we'll find some 'alone time' tonight. If you know what I mean?" He followed it up with his devastating grin.

Oh, I knew what he meant, all right.

Another glare at Max, then Konner planted a passionate kiss on my lips. I got a good taste of the burger he'd just eaten.

After the kiss ended, Konner pinned me with a significant look. "See you tonight, babe."

I smiled back and hoped I didn't look as nervous as I felt. No way was I ready to go as far as Konner was. Why did he have to pressure me now, especially after the cruddy few days I'd had?

Barely aware of Max on my heels, I made my way to psych class, where a brutal test awaited. The morning had shot my confidence to smithereens, so I turned over the test with a feeling of doom. Then I perked up. Questions on Erikson's eight stages of psychosocial development filled the first half of the test. Yes!

Feeling like I'd managed at least a B on the test thanks to Max and his Gestapo drilling methods, I met Hannah by our lockers.

"Morgan, hurry up," she said. "Hsu is posting the election results in the cafeteria right now."

This was it! Excitement surged through me, but there were nerves as well. The *Gadfly's* article could not have come out at a worse time.

Hannah gave me a hug. "You're gonna be our new class president. I just know it."

Good thing I didn't count on Hannah's ESP for reliable information. Because one look at Brittany Whittaker's triumphant smirk as she stood outside the cafeteria told me that she'd been elected the senior class president.

Wearing variations on the same short skirt/tight blouse combo Brittany always sported, her minions fawned around her while she graciously acknowledged their congratulations.

"Morgan, there you are," Brittany cooed when she caught sight of me. "Sorry, sweetie. But Abbotts don't win *all* elections, do they?"

"Considering your 'platform'"—I signed air quotes—"was

clearly the best, it's no surprise."

Brittany's plastic smile turned into a snarl.

Hannah stalked forward, and Brittany's posse flinched. "But you better watch out, Brits, honey, because Morgan and I will make sure you keep your campaign promises."

Brittany dismissed Hannah's words. "You know how politics is. Winning comes first. Keeping promises is"—she waved her hand airily—"as needed. Excuse me, please. I'm late for a meeting with Mrs. Hsu. Oh, and a bit of advice, Morgan. You may be the daughter of the president, but you should know that not all publicity is good publicity."

She laughed, and her posse dutifully echoed as they trailed her on her way to the school's administration wing.

Hannah snorted in disgust. "So now we have to live a whole year under Brittany's despotic rule? Maybe we could stage a coup."

"Worked for Napoleon. Or was it Hitler?" I answered sourly.

"Cheer up, Morgan. Karma's a bitch. It'll bite Brittany on the butt one day—hard."

"I don't believe in karma. If I did, I'd have to believe that karma's taken a huge bite out of me. What did I do to deserve all this trouble right now?"

For once, Hannah didn't have an answer.

Chapter Nine

Somehow I got through the rest of the afternoon, though I was still in shock that I lost the election . . . to Brittany Whittaker! Ugh! Mom always said that in politics, integrity would be rewarded, but no one could argue that Brittany's underhanded ways paid off for her big-time. And her crack about not all publicity being good publicity let me know beyond a shadow of a doubt that she was behind that insane newspaper photo of me.

I was pulling books out of my locker when Max approached. "We're going to bring the Baby Beast up the drive," he told me. "You can wait on the front steps for us."

I slammed the locker door shut. "Don't bring the car inside the gate. I hate that. Besides, I have rehearsal."

"There's press outside school grounds. And a camera crew. I think it's best to get you out of here."

Oh craaaaaap.

Max's face betrayed a trace of sympathy, which I totally didn't want at the moment. "Unless you want to be on the six o'clock news, bringing the car onto private property where the press isn't allowed is the only way to avoid them."

I heaved a sigh. "All right. I'll be out there in ten minutes."

As usual, the sight of the heavily armored black limo with the presidential seal on the door caused a stir. Gawky freshmen crowded on the sidewalk to get a closer look at the car and to take photos with their cell phones.

"Maybe Abbott does think she's hot shit," someone muttered audibly. "Glad I voted for Whittaker," someone else answered.

I hurried down the front steps to the waiting car, pushing my way through the crowd. Just as I reached the door, a mic was thrust in my face.

"How does it feel to be an Abbott and lose an election?"

Surprised, I stopped. A young woman, clearly a Georgetown undergrad, complete with skullcap and nose ring, had breached school property with her dreadlocked cameraman.

Before I could blink, Max was between us. "This is private property," Max said. His voice was just a little scary. "You're breaking the law."

He nodded to an agent from the perimeter detail, who moved in on the cameraman.

The color drained out of the young woman's face. "I . . . I didn't know. . . ."

"It's okay, Agent Jackson." I knew what it was like to break the rules and screw something up. "I'll take the question."

I thought of my mother the day after she lost her very first campaign, running for a seat in the House of Representatives. *Always stay classy in victory,* she'd said, *but most especially in defeat. The voters will remember it next time.*

I took a deep breath. "As everyone who participates in democracy knows, losing is sometimes part of the process. I wish my opponent every success, and I know she'll make a fine senior class president."

God, maybe I really was born to be a politician. Because I just told a whopper of a lie.

Max intervened with an air of someone who'd had his last nerve worn out. "We need to roll," he told me, and shooed me into the car.

"Cute outfit today, Morgan!" the reporter called after me before Max shut the limo's door.

The car swung away from the curb. Outside the gate, crews from nearly every news outlet had camped out. Paparazzi ran after the limo to fire off shots, but they wouldn't get anything through the smoked glass windows.

I slouched into the leather seat, bone weary. Today had been another rough one.

As we approached the White House, Max's wireless com chirped and Max instructed the Secret Service driver to pull

69

around to the south entrance.

"What's going on?" I asked.

"Unwanted media has camped by the north entrance," Max answered. "They're on the street with high-powered cameras trained on the driveway."

"Are you kidding?" I asked. "Why?" Then I knew. They wanted another photo of me wearing a crazy outfit.

"Don't worry," Max answered shortly. "I know another way in."

"You do?" But I didn't have time for more questions. We quickly changed directions and pulled into the south entrance by the White House's press briefing room.

"Are you insane?" I screeched. "The press room's crawling with reporters!"

Max muttered into his com before he turned to me. "I'm hiding you in plain sight, Morgan. By the time they realize you're right under their noses, you'll be gone. Plus it's the fastest way in. But we have to move quickly."

"Okaaaaay." It seemed like a long shot, but I didn't have much choice. The car had already stopped.

I have to give Max his props, because his plan worked like a charm. Before the pool reporters even had a chance to register my presence, I'd slipped through them.

Max escorted me to the back stairs leading to the third-floor residence.

"I'll leave you here," he said. "Can I get you to promise you won't make any unauthorized excursions outside of secured areas?"

"Like I'd give the press another shot at getting a horrible photo of me? Not a chance." I slung my backpack on my shoulder and started up the stairs. Then I paused. "Thanks for everything today, Max. You really came through for me."

To my surprise, he stalked away without another word. What was up with him?

Upstairs in the family quarters, nineties grunge rock music blared from the workout room. Dad was home.

"Puddin' Pop, can you come in here?" Dad yelled before I had a chance to sneak past.

I cringed at hearing the nickname Dad would probably be calling me for the rest of my life. An image of me at the ripe old age of sixty flashed through my mind as my ninety-year-old father called me Puddin' Pop from his hovercraft wheelchair.

"Can you turn down the moldy oldies?" I asked as I entered the workout room.

Dad set down the barbell he'd been pumping—he needed to keep in shape for all the surfing he liked to do—and ran his hand over the touchscreen pad of the high-tech sound system invented by Abbott Technology. The guitar riff mercifully died. Dad wiped his sweaty face with a workout towel. His black hair still curled thick and only a couple of lines creased the corners of his eyes.

"Puddin' Pop, I know today must've been rough for you," Dad began.

"You saw the paper?"

"Of course. Your mother is outraged. So am I. The *Gadfly* crossed a line when they went after you."

"Reporters were waiting for me at the school gates today."

He got up off the weight bench and gave me a sweaty hug. "I know this is tough, but believe me when I say this will pass. Remember what happened during the campaign when Mom was ready to secure the nomination? The coconut bra incident?"

I nodded miserably. Someone had found photos from Dad's days as a fraternity brother in college. Photos of him in a grass hula skirt and coconut bra at some frat kegger got splashed over the front page of every major newspaper from coast to coast. "Bra-gate" almost cost Mom the nomination.

"I know that sucked, Dad, but it's not the same. You chose to marry a politician and run the risk of looking like an idiot in public. I didn't ask for all this attention and it's ruining my life!"

At that moment, Dad's cell phone, tossed onto a pile of his martial arts uniforms, began to vibrate. Dad gave me a hard look before reaching for it. "It's your mother," he said, reading the text message. "She wants to speak to you."

"Where is she?"

"Oval Office."

I sighed. I wanted to whine that I was always going to her instead of her coming to me, but even I knew that maintaining world peace was going to be the trump card every time.

"Hang in there, Puddin' Pop." Dad gave me an encouraging smile as I trudged out.

Inside the executive assistant's office, Padma's eyes were glued to the flat-panel TV mounted on the wall.

"Omigod!" A montage of unflattering photos of me flashed on the screen. There I was as a kid in my ballet tutu and braces. The photo was overlaid by the one of me in my *Rent* costume, boobs ahoy.

Padma hurriedly clicked off the TV. "Wait here just a sec, Morgan. I'll see if your mom is ready for you."

"Thanks." I didn't ask for any toffees this time. I felt vaguely like throwing up.

"It's unforgivable!" I heard Mom saying angrily when Padma opened the connecting door to the Oval Office.

I peeked. Mom paced furiously over the eagle's seal on the rug. I'd never seen her so livid. Standing at attention near Washington's portrait, Humberto Morales, Mom's chief of staff, looked concerned.

"I want the *Gadfly*'s press pass pulled for a start, Humberto." Mom's voice sliced; I'm surprised Humberto didn't split in two.

"Then I want any paper that reprints the photo to be officially reprimanded. No interviews, no access, none of their reporters allowed on Air Force One or Two. Understood?"

"I'm not sure that's the wisest course, Sara—"

"They crossed a line when they went after Morgan. I will not have it."

"I agree that Morgan is off-limits to press, but let's do this the right way." Humberto held his hand up in a conciliatory gesture. "You can't afford any further slips in the polls. I'll send surrogates out to the Sunday talk shows to express our displeasure about this outrageous breach of Morgan's privacy. We'll push our side to friendly bloggers and have editorials hit the major papers. Spun the right way, we'll be able to protect Morgan from future breaches and gain public sympathy."

"I don't give a damn about public sympathy, I want the harassment to stop!"

Padma's voice murmured. Mom put a hand to her forehead and took a deep breath. "Do I look calm?" she said to Padma. "Okay, send her in."

Truth was, Mom looked anything but calm.

Chapter Ten

When that fire lit Mom's eyes, watch out.

"Come on in, honey." Visibly, she pulled herself together. As I entered the Oval Office, Humberto gave me a friendly nod then faded into the shadowy hallways of the West Wing. Humberto was a cool guy, but he was short on chitchat. That's probably why Mom kept him on her staff during her transition from the Senate to the presidency.

Mom beckoned me over to the sofa and turned to Padma. "Why don't you ask the kitchen to send up a snack? Some of Nigel's gingersnaps should get Morgan and me through the afternoon."

"You got it, Sara." Padma shut the door behind her.

I plopped on the couch and Mom sat next to me. "I'm so sorry about all this, Morgan. But I promise I'll do everything in my power to get the press off your back."

"Yeah. Okay."

She brushed a lock of hair from my forehead the way she used to when I was little. "You're growing up. I didn't really realize until I saw that photo in the *Gadfly*."

"Mom, gross! Those are gel enhancers! Hannah used them for my costume."

"No kidding? Maybe Hannah could let me borrow a couple, and I'll send your father out in his coconut bra to the next National Press Club luncheon. That'd really give them a story."

"Don't even think about it. You know he'd totally do it!"

Mom laughed a hearty honk of a laugh. I hadn't heard one of those from her in I don't know how long. "We could put the photo on our Christmas cards. The party donors would have a heart attack."

"So would Nana."

We busted up. Nana Abbott came from a starchy Connecticut blue-blood line. Every teapot wore its cozy at Nana Abbott's house.

A chirping cut across our laughter, and the red button on the phone on Mom's desk blinked.

Instantly, Mom switched into president mode, and rose. "I have to take this call, honey. Just a minute."

"No prob." I'd gotten used to getting my mom's attention in bits and pieces over the years.

She snatched the phone off its cradle. "Sara Abbott here."

Padma came in with a tray of cookies, a pot of coffee for

Mom, and a soda for me. Reluctantly I took a gingersnap and nibbled. I didn't want to spoil my appetite before my date with Konner tonight, but Nigel's cookies were too amazing to pass up. He'd drizzled dark chocolate over this batch.

While I ate, I listened to fragments of Mom's phone conversation.

"I'm not signing the bill if Congress loads more pork-barrel spending in it," Mom said. "Tell the speaker of the House that the bill will be DOA if I see one more congressional pet project attached to it."

Mom said she found it ironic that when she was in Congress, she thought the president didn't compromise enough. Now that she's the president, she feels that she compromises too much.

I was reaching for another gingersnap when Sally Kempton, Mom's rail-thin, chain-smoking communications director, tapped on the door and opened it. "Press conference in thirty minutes," she mouthed from the doorway.

Mom nodded without missing a beat in her phone conversation. Three seconds later, she'd hung up. "Why don't you come with me?" she said, sliding her arms into the suit jacket she'd draped over the back of her chair.

"Really?" Mom never asked me to go to presidential press conferences—not after that time she caught me snoozing while she gave her stump speech. It wasn't my fault; I'd already heard the speech a gazillion times when we'd been on the campaign trail.

"It would be great to have you in my corner. Abbotts have to stick together, don't we?"

As much as I wanted to be angry with her, to blame her for this mess, I couldn't help but feel a little—okay a lot—proud of my mom. "Yeah. We do."

I followed Mom to the Brady Press Briefing Room. The sight of camera crews and reporters milling about made my stomach automatically lurch, and I hurried after Mom into the peanut-sized green room where Humberto was waiting.

I twirled in the makeup chair while Mom and Humberto huddled in the corner and went over last-minute talking points. Dion, Mom's makeup artist, walked in and came toward me. "Okay, Sara—oh gosh! Morgan? Sorry, hon."

"That's okay. I'm getting that a lot lately. Must be the hair." Honestly, tomorrow I was going to get the bob hairstyle cut off. Shaved off. Whatever it took.

"Well, I'm going to take it as a compliment," Mom said with a smile, shooing me out of the makeup chair. Humberto seemed to have vanished. He has this way of being everywhere and nowhere. It's kind of freaky, actually.

Dion got out the makeup brushes and a can of hairspray. "You should, Sara. You and Morgan could be twins."

"It's nice to know I won't need any Botox injections for a while," Mom joked.

"Everyone take a deep breath," Dion warned, and sprayed Mom's hair with a cloud of aerosol.

After the coughing subsided, Humberto poked his head in. "They're ready, Sara."

"Showtime." Mom stood up. She straightened her shoulders, and suddenly Mom disappeared and I was looking at the president of the United States.

In the crowded press briefing room, cameras and video monitors whirred while reporters peppered Mom with questions. From my seat in the wings, I got a good view of the media circus. I recognized a few of the reporters. Mom answered even the most aggressive reporters calmly, and I marveled at how she kept her cool. From her position at the blue lectern bearing the presidential seal, Mom pointed to reporter after reporter, careful to give each one a chance to ask a question.

"Yes, Helen?" Mom pointed to an older woman wearing an outrageous yellow-checkerboard suit.

"Chet Whittaker made good on his threat to kill your micro-loan program for those below the poverty line. What are your plans for the initiative now?"

Ah, the Whittakers. Brits, my nemesis, and Chet, the leader of the opposition party.

"To try again," Mom responded firmly. "The opposition party feels that money spent on the poor is money wasted. We feel differently. Next session we'll work harder to convince the congressional delegates that this legislation is needed. Tom?"

Tom Agoletti of *The New York Times* rose. "There's been criticism of your administration's new offshore drilling regulations. The oil companies in particular have launched a media blitz against it. Will you hold hearings on the issue?"

Mom rubbed her ear. I could tell she didn't like the question. "Change is always hard at first, Tom. We feel confident that the CEOs of the Big Three oil companies will agree that reworking our country's energy policy is the right thing to do."

It occurred to me that Mom just gave one of her famous (the opposition party would call it infamous) non-answer answers.

"Yes, Jerry?" she said to her least favorite reporter from *The Washington Post.*

Jerry Shutz stood and stabbed his pen aggressively at Mom. "President Abbott, the situation in the African tidal basin is getting more fragile. General Mfuso's ruling military junta has threatened civil war unless the opposition party gives up its demand for free elections. There are also rumors that Mfuso has purchased a supply of yellowcake uranium. What is the American response to the threats?"

Mom cocked her head to one side. "We shall protect our strategic interests in the region. But diplomacy is always our first resort. I'm confident we'll reach an accord between General Mfuso and Bishop Welak of the Democratic People's Army. Then we can bring peace to the region."

Chairs scraped, papers rustled. The press conference was wrapping up.

"Do you have any comment about your daughter's picture in today's *Gadfly*?" someone called out.

Mom's brown eyes zapped the room. "It was an outrageous breach of my daughter's privacy. I'll remind all of you that she is an eighteen-year-old girl. How would you feel if that happened to your daughter? I'll tell you how you would feel—furious!"

The press room went uncomfortably silent.

Mom nodded to Humberto and stepped away from the lectern. Reporters rose from their chairs. The press conference was over.

"Wow, Mom, you spanked them hard," I said admiringly as we took a shortcut through the Cabinet Room on our way back to Mom's office.

"No one harasses my kid and gets away with it." She wrapped her arm around my waist and we strolled past the long oval table that Mom and her Cabinet staff sat around while they decided the fate of the world.

Mom paused in front of the door connecting the Cabinet Room to the Oval Office. "Hard-won experience tells me this kerfuffle will blow over soon . . . but . . ."

Mom paused.

I tensed. She was getting ready to drop a bomb.

". . . do you think you could back out of the musical?"

"What!?" My voice rose to a screech. "But I've been working on it for weeks now!"

"You know I hate to ask it," Mom said hastily. "But even though we're doing what we can with respect to the media, I'm worried they'll still find a way to disrupt the performance. Or worse, drag your classmates into the bad publicity. You know we can't control everything."

"I know," I muttered.

"I just don't want you to be the target of any more negative press. Or compromising photos. They will follow you around for the rest of your life."

"I'll think about it." Part of me knew that Mom was right. I didn't want the media to ruin the show and I'd hate it if reporters dug up dirt on one of the other cast members or printed some crazy photo. But the other part of me stubbornly refused to go there. I'd worked hard on my role, and I didn't want to give it up.

Mom gave me her special megawatt smile. "Thanks, sweetie. You go ahead in. I'll be back in a minute; I forgot that I have to check something with Humberto. Have another gingersnap."

My stomach growled. Why did she have to mention the cookies? And why did she have to ask me to give up the musical? Drama was the only thing I was good at. I needed something in my life that I didn't totally screw up.

Inside the Oval Office, I snatched another gingersnap off

the tray and trudged to the three floor-length windows behind Mom's desk. The window right behind the desk sported a killer view of Capitol Hill's white dome gleaming gold in the afternoon sun.

I munched the gingersnap and thought about Mom's request. I ran a hand over the surface of the Resolute Desk where Mom signed executive orders that changed the fate of the world— and here I was upset about backing out of some stupid school musical even though my presence could put my classmates in jeopardy with the press. The welfare of others comes first.

I sat in the leather chair and tried to imagine what it would be like to be the president of the United States with the unlimited power of a mighty nation at my fingertips. Wars ended, humanitarian aid rendered, stock market crashes averted—hey, look, Mom kept a tube of Mentos in her desk drawer. . . .

I put my feet up on the desk's surface and popped a mint. *If I were the president, what would I do . . . ?*

I'd outlaw the color pink and anything else that reminded me of Brittany. Perhaps I'd have the FBI investigate "Speech Gate." It's got to be illegal to snag someone's class-president speech, right? I'd make Hannah the nation's style ambassador. And I'd ban lilies so I could be safe from sneezing fits.

I giggled. That would be a gross abuse of presidential power, for sure.

The phone on Mom's desk rang. The LCD screen flashed

COS Room for the chief of staff's office. Probably Mom checking on me from Humberto's office.

I cleared my throat and picked up the line. Let's see if I could freak Mom out. "Sara Abbott here."

"Sara, we've got a problem." Humberto's voice carried a sense of urgency. "It's Mfuso again. He's threatening to move his troops to seal the border if we continue talks with Bishop Welak—"

"Hold up, Humberto. It's me—Morgan!"

"Morgan?"

I felt myself go hot. He was going to kill me! "I . . . I thought it was Mom calling me, and I wanted to play a joke on her. I'm really sorry."

Silence. Then: "You really sounded just like her. Where is she?"

"I thought she was with you. Please don't tell her what I did, Humberto. I don't need any more trouble today."

"I won't tell if you promise not to answer the Oval Office phone again, okay?"

"You got it."

I hung up and heaved a sigh of relief. Humberto was first and foremost loyal to my mom, but he kept his promises. And there would be no problem holding up my end of the bargain. That brush with Mom's reality scared the bejeezus out of me. I didn't want to know half the stuff that went on around here.

Padma tapped on the door and entered. "Morgan, your

mom's been called away to an emergency session with the Joint Chiefs. She apologizes, but she'll be gone for a few hours."

Disappointment flooded me. Then anger. Mom couldn't pick up her cell phone and call me herself? She knew I was waiting for her. I couldn't believe she sent Pads to dismiss me like I was some deputy aide.

I stalked out of the Oval Office. I tried to tell myself that the president had responsibilities to the country. But I couldn't help being resentful. It's like everyone else came first. For a moment during the press conference, it felt like Mom had made me her priority. But just like that, I'd gone straight to the bottom of her list again.

Max waited for me in the West Colonnade overlooking the Rose Garden, where I was about to leave the protective zone of security in the West Wing. His sky-blue shirt set off his eyes, and I had to admit he looked pretty good for a Secret Service agent.

I gave Max a nod and tried to forget about, well, everything. "Wassup, Ball and Chain?"

Max's lips twitched. "The advance team just came back from a sweep of that sushi bar you want to go to tonight . . . hey, is anything wrong? You look upset."

"No. Yeah. Nothing." Guess I wasn't that great of an actress. "Just the whole daughter of the president thing."

"Like what?" he asked as we continued walking.

"Not only did my mom blow me off for a meeting that just happened to crop up 'unexpectedly,' but she asked me to give up something really important." I felt sick when I even thought about the musical now. "She thinks being in AOP's drama production will bring more bad publicity."

He paused before responding, "She's probably right, don't you think?"

"Yeah, and that just makes me angrier. Why is she always right?"

"She *is* the president," he answered.

"You think I've forgotten? I've been taking a backseat to the presidency ever since she got elected."

"Hey." Max stopped my headlong charge through the Cross Hall. "Your mom is making decisions that can affect the lives of millions of people. Maybe even the survival of the planet. Why don't you cut her some slack?"

"Are you lecturing me on how to feel now, Agent Jackson? I'm not allowed to get ticked when my mother sloughs me off? I thought one of Erikson's stages of psychosocial development was a sense of individuality. Well, this individual is pissed off."

Max's blue eyes held mine for a moment. "You don't know how lucky you are to have a mother like yours, Morgan. Maybe someday you'll understand."

The silence between us went on a beat too long.

"I gotta get ready for my date tonight," I said. "Konner doesn't like it when I'm late."

"I bet he doesn't." Max headed down the hall toward the motorpool to get the Baby Beast ready, and I headed upstairs to my room.

Chapter Eleven

Something about the way he said "I bet" in relation to Konner bugged me.

I was about to call down to the motorpool to ask if a different agent could escort me and Konner to the sushi bar when my cell phone bleated.

"It's Mr. Escobedo, Morgan. You weren't at rehearsal today."

Ulp.

"Everything all right?" he continued. I could tell he was trying to hide his annoyance.

I took a deep breath. I couldn't believe what I was about to say, but Max's words about my mom rang in my ears.

"Uh, I'm really sorry about this, Mr. Escobedo, but I have to drop out of the production."

The silence on the other end of the line was way worse than one of his yelling fits.

"My mom thinks that my recent negative publicity is going

to adversely impact the musical." There, that sounded pretty professional. Even if it was killing me to say.

"It's a theatrical production at a high school. Surely the press has better things to do than to breach security at AOP for a candid shot of the president's daughter."

"You'd think."

"Well, I'll give your role to the understudy. Though I wish you would have let me know you were dropping out today so she could have had a decent dress rehearsal before the curtain goes up."

"I'm sorry, Mr. Escobedo, but it's not my fault—"

"The show goes on, Morgan. With or without you."

He beeped off. I threw my phone on the bed. That. Sucked.

Thank god Hannah would be here soon. She'd promised to come over and help me get ready for my date with Konner. I took a hot shower and tried to ignore the hole in my chest over giving up the musical.

I'd just finished moisturizing my legs and plucking a few stray hairs out of my brows when Hannah finally showed up.

"Where've you been?" I asked.

"Blame your hunky Secret Service agent." Hannah unloaded a curling iron, hairclips, and a can of hairspray from her massive handbag. I half expected her to haul a hairdresser's sink out of there, too. "He wanted me to sign into the White House visitor's log, then he had to scan my bag for bombs or anthrax. Took forever."

"Sorry, Han, he's driving me crazy." Hannah listened to me vent about the three Ms causing me grief: Mom, the musical, and Max. She crimped my hair out of its boring blunt cut and wove it into a mystifyingly awesome cloud of curls.

She tucked jeweled butterfly clips here and there among them. "Konner's not gonna be able to take his eyes off you tonight!"

"It's not his eyes that I'm worried about."

Hannah suddenly got really interested in one of the clips. "Is he pressuring you?"

"No. Well, I mean, yes. I guess so. I really like him, and he's so gorgeous. But sometimes he . . . makes me uncomfortable."

"Then you have to tell him to stop. Don't let him sweet-talk you into anything you don't want to do."

"I don't want to lose him."

"I don't care how popular Konner Tippington *thinks* he is, he has to respect you."

"Konner respects me," I answered hotly.

"Well, I don't trust the boy. After four years watching him in action at AOP, I can safely say that Konner's world revolves around Konner."

"Hey, that's pretty harsh."

"I'm not sugarcoating it for you, Morgan. But he's your

boyfriend, not mine. Now come on. It's almost seven o'clock and you're not even dressed."

I dropped it because I didn't want to hear what other thoughts Hannah held on the subject of Konner, and truthfully, I was tired of arguing with the whole world.

Hannah had taken my paisley wrap dress and added some retro fringe to the sleeves. It was amazing. She also let me borrow her knee-high suede boots, then I topped the whole outfit off with a macramé wrap we'd found in a D.C. thrift shop.

"Wow." In the full-length mirror, I gazed at myself in wonder. Was that me? The dress hugged my curves, and the boots' stiletto heels added inches to my height to make me seem willowy.

Hannah studied me critically. "Yep, I'm good."

I sashayed down the back stairwell feeling like a supermodel, Hannah following. Max was waiting at the bottom of the stairs, muttering into his com.

"Is the car ready?" I asked from the second step.

Max turned. His eyes widened. "Yeah. I mean, yes."

"Great."

He didn't move.

Hannah and I exchanged glances. "Maybe we should, like, go or something," I added, eager to dispel the tingly feeling that shot through my stomach when I realized that I'd rendered Max speechless.

He swallowed. Hard. Then he said into his mic: "Tornado's

ready to leave the farm. Pull the Beast around."

I gave Hannah a hug. "Remember what we talked about," she whispered. "Don't let Konner pressure you into anything you don't want to do."

"He won't," I whispered back. "Konner's sensitive."

Hannah stopped an eyeroll just in time.

Max kept his gaze firmly out the window as we drove to Georgetown to pick up Konner.

When my boyfriend stepped out of his house, my heart beat a little bit faster. With his blond hair gelled back and the collar of his crisp blue shirt opened at his muscular throat, he looked like a model. He was perfect, and he went out with *me*.

"Whoa, babe, you look hot tonight." Konner slid next to me in the limo and gave my thigh a squeeze. "Tonight's gonna be great."

"I think so, too," I murmured, careful to keep my voice down so Max couldn't hear. For some reason, I was uncomfortable with Max overhearing my conversation with Konner.

Konner pulled me super close and started nuzzling my hair. "Mmm, you smell good."

I drew away a tad, already feeling the pressure. "Thanks."

D.C. at night glimmered magically as we drove into Adams Morgan, where the best ethnic restaurants in D.C. could be found—killer Korean barbecues, Ethiopian mesobs. As we approached Mikyasa, I noticed a crowd of people milling in front of the restaurant.

"What's going on?" I asked. Then I spotted the cameras with high-powered lenses attached. "Oh god. It's paparazzi!"

Konner straightened the front of his shirt. "How do I look?"

"Max!" I gave my Secret Service agent an agonized look.

Max was already chattering into his wireless mic to the advance detail in the restaurant.

The limo slowed curbside. People started flowing toward the car, waving their cameras and snapping photos.

Max chirped off his com. "Word leaked, Morgan. Do you want to cancel?"

I looked at Konner. He didn't seem bothered by the media attention. *Enthralled* would be a better word.

"It'll be okay," I said reluctantly.

Max nodded. He mumbled into his com again. Suddenly a phalanx of Secret Service agents emerged from the sushi bar and cleared a path from the doorway to the limo.

"Wow, it's just like a red carpet," Konner said. "C'mon, babe."

Konner grabbed my hand and yanked me out of the limo. I nearly twisted my ankle in Hannah's boots. Konner flashed a smile as paparazzi snapped photos and shouted, "Morgan, look here! Thanks, honey! Morgan, where's your bustier and hot pants? Morgan, Morgan, Morgan . . ."

Mom always said it was important not to look blindsided when confronted with unexpected media, even though you've been, uh, blindsided. I raised my head with a confidence I didn't feel, and smiled at the crush of photographers. Cameras whirred and clicked.

Max, grim faced, herded us through the line to the door. Just as we reached it, I felt my hair being tugged. Someone snatched away a butterfly clip and a curl fell across my face. I hurried along, hoping more of my clips wouldn't be ripped off my head only to end up at auction on eBay.

The door shut behind us. All eyes from the patrons in the restaurant turned our way.

"Yo, that was awesome!" Konner exclaimed.

I felt like we'd just run an army obstacle course. "Let's just sit down."

Konner grinned and gave a *wassup* nod to the other restaurant patrons as Max ushered us to our seats at the sushi bar before melting into the background a discreet distance away. No way did I want to sit under the full glare of the bar's track lighting. Paparazzi were still trying to take shots through the window of the restaurant; the last thing I needed was a front-page photo of me macking on a California roll.

Konner got a little sulky when I asked if we could have a back table instead. "It's too dark back here," he said.

"That's the point." Since Konner wasn't doing it, I unwound

the macramé wrap from my shoulders and draped it along the back of the chair before sitting down.

Konner's attention immediately zoomed on my cleavage. "Maybe after dinner we can take a stroll along the Mall. You know, to 'look at the lights.'" He gave me a big wink-wink.

"Shh. Keep your voice down." I peered over my shoulder.

"Why?"

"Because I don't want anyone tipping off the media. You know the situation. I can't risk another scandalous headline." Though I'd love to do something spontaneous like take a walk with Konner among the breathtakingly beautiful monuments on the Mall, I got cold chills thinking about Mom opening the *Gadfly* and seeing the headline: MORGAN ABBOTT MAKES OUT WITH BOYFRIEND AT JEFFERSON MEMORIAL.

Konner grabbed my hand and started planting slobbery kisses on my wrist. "I'll make it worth the risk."

I tried to ease my hand away. "Come on, Konner. Everyone can see us."

"So?" He tightened his grip on me and something close to anger flashed in the back of his eyes.

I wrenched my hand away. "Just cool it."

Konner slumped back in his seat, arms crossed. "Fine. Let's order."

"Konner—"

"Drop it."

I did. But I felt awful.

The mood between us soured. All through the tempura and sushi rolls, I plastered on a smile and kept a stream of light chatter going, but it got harder and harder. Konner's sulk deepened to scowling silence by the time the kimono-clad waitress served the green-tea ice cream.

"We can still take a drive along the Mall as long as we don't get out of the car," I said, trying to appease him.

"And have your Secret Service agent watch us make out? No, thanks."

"How about going back to the White House movie theater? My dad ordered the new James Bond movie—we can see it before anyone else in America does—"

"You know what? I think I'll take a cab home instead."

The spoonful of ice cream froze on its way to my mouth. "What?"

"I said, I'll take a cab home, Morgan. The atmosphere will be less *frigid*, if you catch my drift."

I stared at him, speechless.

"I'm sick of having a girlfriend who drags her Secret Service agent along on a date," he continued. "And who can't take a walk with her boyfriend because she's afraid of the bad publicity."

"Are you breaking up with me?"

"Yeah. I guess I am."

"All right." Carefully I folded the napkin on my lap and set it next to my bowl of melted ice cream. A painful lump formed in my throat, but I swallowed it down. Konner had every right to break up with me. But I thought he could at least be honest. I knew it wasn't the media attention that he was sick of. It was the fact that I wasn't letting him get past first base.

I signaled to Max, who was waiting in the shadows of the wait station.

"I'll have one of the agents call you a cab," I said with a graciousness I didn't feel, conscious of potentially prying ears at the nearby tables. "Thank you so much for the lovely evening. It was very . . . special."

"Whatever," Konner mumbled. He didn't look up from his folded arms.

"See you around." I rose and went around the table to give him a kiss on the cheek. He didn't respond.

When I straightened up, Max was waiting with my wrap. He placed it around my shoulders without a word and I leaned into him. I was glad to be ushered out of the restaurant before the first tears spilled. As soon as I was inside the safety of the limo with its tinted windows, I let them fly. I knew I was crying about more than losing Konner, though. The last two days had been horrible and it was all catching up with me.

A tissue appeared in my hand. "Thanks, Max," I gulped, and scrubbed at my wet cheeks.

"I've got a whole box here if you need them."

He placed the tissues next to me on the leather seat. I expected him to say something inane about how life goes on, yada yada. But he didn't. What he said was: "It's his loss, Morgan."

He buzzed the driver up front to take the long way home, and let me bawl.

Chapter Twelve

Midnight came and went on my googly-eyed digital clock
before I admitted that I wasn't getting to sleep anytime soon. I'd
only eaten three bites of California roll and a nibble of tempura
at the sushi bar. Now that my crying jag had ended—thanks to
a reassuring emergency phone call to Hannah—and resignation
over Konner dumping me set in, my stomach kicked at me. I
needed a snack.

I ran into Nigel shelving a hotel pan in the walk-in
refrigerator. "What are you doing here so late?" I asked.

"'Allo, Morgan. Shouldn't I ask you the same thing?"

"I'm just getting a snack. You?"

"Your mum's hosting a banquet for the American Business
Leadership Council in a little over a week. I thought we'd
go Caribbean for that one. Conch soup, shredded pork with
coconut garnish. The whole works."

"Sounds yummy."

"I never get time to experiment during the day and I need a few days to order the ingredients in bulk once my recipes are perfected. Do you have a minute to try a tropical fruit salad? It's a new recipe and it's not quite right, I'm afraid. I need a fresh palate to tell me which direction to go."

"Mine's pretty fresh right now." As soon as he said "tropical fruit," my mouth started to water.

The mango, papaya, and cilantro worked wonderfully together. "But it needs a kick," I told him. "Maybe a jalapeño pepper?"

Nigel took a mouthful of the fruit and nodded. "Heat—that's exactly what's missing. A few drops of scotch bonnet essence would work and stay within the theme. Thanks, luv. You're becoming quite the gourmand, you know."

"Gourmand?"

"Foodie."

"Aww, thanks, Nige." Nigel Bellingham was the best chef in the country. Getting a compliment like that from him was really something.

I surveyed the piles of coconut shells, banana leaves, and other exotic ingredients heaped on the stainless steel countertops. "How much is this thing setting back the annual budget?" I asked idly while I popped another chunk of papaya in my mouth.

"With wine, about three hundred dollars per person."

"Yikes! You're kidding, right? That's outrageous!"

"Well, we can't serve the titans of industry Ding Dongs and Cheez Doodles, can we?"

Point taken. Still, my mind spun at how much money the whole banquet would cost.

I sipped a cup of Nigel's special cinnamon-spiced hot chocolate and flipped on the kitchen TV. The laughter from the live audience at *LateNite Skits* (or LateNite Skewer, as Dad called it) blared into the kitchen. I giggled at a Harry Potter spoof.

The next skit opened with one of the comediennes dressed in a bustier and PVC hot pants bounding into a set that looked suspiciously like the White House's Oval Office. "Hi, America! I'm Morgan Abbott, and I'm here to talk to you about the dangers of plastic clothing—"

Oh. My. God.

Frozen with horror, I watched the comedienne's gel enhancers burst into flames. When did I become a national joke?

My late-night munchies vanished. I clicked the TV off. "I'm heading back up, Nigel," I called to him. To put a pillow over my face. And possibly die of embarrassment.

A muffled answer came out of the pantry. "Righto, Morgan. Thanks for your help tonight."

"No biggie."

Even after midnight, the White House buzzed with staff, cleaning crews, and ever-present security. I gave the straight-faced marine guarding the entrance to the West Wing a nod of acknowledgment as I passed him, even though he wasn't allowed to respond.

I breathed a sigh of relief that in front of the Palm Room, which connected the West Wing to the White House residence, someone had swapped the vase of white lilies with roses. A sneezing jag was the last thing I needed. I was ready to pull the covers over my head and end this rotten day.

Just then, the door to the Palm Room opened, and my mom swept out with an entourage of aides and Cabinet members surrounding her. Her mouth was pursed in a way I recognized, and I knew she was holding back her temper. She walked so rapidly, her aides puffed to keep up with her.

Yep. Mom was pissed off about something.

The marine and I exchanged looks. "Let's just hope she doesn't take it out on Canada," I joked, and headed up to my room.

When I woke the next morning, I still felt rotten. Maybe it had gotten a little worse, actually, which was weird for me, because once I managed to drag myself out of bed I was usually ready to rock and roll.

By around seven a.m., when I should've been goofing with my hair and demolishing a bowl of Cap'n Crunch, Dad tapped on my bedroom door and stuck his head in. "What's going on,

Puddin' Pop? Why aren't you ready for school? Are you sick?"

I groaned and rolled over on my side. "You could say that. Sick of having a bad day."

"Come on, honey. Everyone has bad days."

"Let's see. In the last two days, I've lost an election I'd worked really hard on, a horrible photo of me has become the most popular download in the history of Celebricity.com, my boyfriend broke up with me, I had to quit the musical for national security reasons, I'm a staple on sketch comedy shows, and Mom says I'm grounded if I don't get my grades up. And I think I got Denny fired, but I can't be totally sure of that."

"Denny's fine, Morgan—he's just on vacation. But your ability to pack a lot of trouble into a short amount of time is highly developed."

"Har-di-har-har." I threw a sheet over my head.

"C'mon, Morgan." I felt the edge of the mattress sag. Dad eased the covers back down.

Dad was wearing his charcoal-gray suit he'd had made in London, which made his tan look fantastic. He'd shaved his goatee when Mom started running for the presidency, but nothing could shake his overall air of Cali business cool.

"The best way to solve problems—"

"—is to face them head-on. I know that, Dad. But facing this many problems could mean I'd be run over, killed, or at the very least maimed. Honestly."

He patted my bed head. "All right, Morgan. I'll tell your mom that you can stay home today. But put it to good use hitting the books."

"I will."

He rose. "And come Monday, you walk through school with your head high and your integrity intact. Remember, if you keep living life on your terms, people can mock it all they want, but they'll respect you in the end."

"I'll try to remember." Good lord, the man had read too many business management books.

He kissed my forehead. "I'll be in London for the ribbon cutting of Abbott Tech's European division for the next week or so, but I'm only a phone call away."

"Thanks, Dad."

I did feel better. Sometimes a girl needed a pep talk from her father.

I'd just finished eating a bowl of cereal in bed and scrolling through my MP3 playlist (no way was I turning on the TV today), when Mom came in, wearing silk pajamas. "Dad told me you're staying home from school," she began.

"Yeah. It's a mental health day."

Mom grinned and scooted me over on the bed so she could sit next to me. "What I wouldn't give for one of those myself."

"Rough couple days?"

"I've had worse." She slung her arm around my shoulders

and gave me a hug. I remembered when Mom used to wake me every morning with a kiss and a cuddle. Then she became the president, and I grew up.

Still, this was nice.

"How was your dinner with Konner?" she asked.

"Not so good. He broke up with me last night."

"Ouch."

"Yeah. He says he's sick of dating a girl who has to drag Secret Service agents everywhere."

"He never seemed to have a problem with it before."

I shrugged. "Then I made the mistake of watching *LateNight Skits*."

"Humberto is already calling the head of the network."

"Thanks, Mom." I leaned into her, smelling her jasmine-scented lotion and feeling a lot better.

"Maybe I should send the CIA on a special mission to Konner's house," Mom said. "Operation Morgan's Revenge. Atomic wedgies—Special Ops style."

We giggled together.

"I think I still sorta like Konner," I said reluctantly. "But I wouldn't say no to the FBI sneaking glue into his bottle of hair gel."

Mom honked in laughter, and I joined in.

Suddenly I realized that it was after eight a.m. "Shouldn't you be at the office now?" I asked.

"I should. But I've had a cancellation. My schedule's open for the next few hours."

A cancellation? Who cancels on the president of the United States? "What's really going on?"

When she hesitated, I pressed her. "You can trust me, Mom. Once your cleavage has been mocked on national TV, you can handle anything."

"You're right. You're growing up so fast, sweetie. Sometimes I forget. Truth is, there's been a setback in plans for the African peace accords. I won't be going to Africa."

"But you've been working on it for months. I thought there had been a breakthrough."

"We did, too. But now the military juntas are making impossible demands. Last night the skirmishes broke out again, and the CIA says that the region is slipping back into chaos. The meetings have been canceled, mostly because the security situation is so fragile."

"You mean the CIA and Secret Service won't be able to protect you if you go."

"Bingo."

I gave my mom a hard hug. I never got used to the ever-present security threats surrounding her. Too many presidents have been assassinated for me not to take them seriously. "Then I'm glad you're not going. I'm sorry for those people, but it's too dangerous for you."

"I know. But I'm frustrated that things are stalled. More lives will be lost. Years of economic progress down the drain. What a waste."

"But you tried."

"Trying's not enough, sweetie. The president must show results. I've already been criticized for not being strong in foreign affairs, despite my lifelong training as a diplomat."

True. Mom's family, the Fortescues, had all become legendary diplomats. Great-grandpa Fortescue, Mom's grandfather, had been instrumental in bringing Stalin and Roosevelt together at the end of World War II.

"I really wanted this peace initiative to work out," Mom continued. "Then I could prove to the American people that I'm just as strong in foreign affairs as domestic. Plus, there's . . ." Her voice trailed away.

A chill crawled up my spine. This Africa situation was way more serious than I thought. "What's going on?"

Mom's eyes refocused on me. She forced a smile as she touched my hair. "You've become a beautiful young woman, you know that? Everyone's child should grow up in a peaceful country, not just my child."

Now I was freaking out even more. Mom never talked like that. "Does this have something to do with the uranium that the *Washington Post* reporter was talking about at the press conference yesterday?"

"How did you—?"

"C'mon, Mom. My GPA may be a teeny bit on the low side, but I know how to put two and two together."

She hesitated. Then she nodded. "It's yellowcake uranium but that's classified information, Morgan."

I barely heard her. Even with my primitive grasp of chemistry, I knew that uranium was used to make nuclear bombs.

"I really needed this meeting with Mfuso and Welak to happen," Mom went on. "If I could just get them in the same room, I know I could broker a peace deal and persuade Mfuso to hand over the yellowcake. He wants to deal with me and only me—not my secretary of state. I'm sure he thinks that negotiating with a woman will gain him more concessions."

Part of my brain was thinking *Good luck with that, Mfuso.* Mom didn't give away anything she didn't want to. The other part was entertaining an impossible possibility. . . .

"Now that the meeting's been canceled, I'm twiddling my thumbs for the next few days. Damn!" Mom drove her fist in her palm.

Her disappointment and frustration were palpable. The idea forming in the back of my mind started to take shape. "So you have nothing public scheduled for the next few days?"

"Nope."

"How long do you think you'd need to get General Mfuso and Bishop Welak together at the negotiating table?"

"A week, probably. Less, even, given the right incentives for Mfuso. And I know exactly what he wants. The tricky part is getting Bishop Welak to agree, but Welak doesn't want a nuclear disaster on his hands any more than the rest of us do."

"The situation is that serious?"

"It is."

My heart began beating quickly. I could hardly believe what I was about to suggest. "Why don't you let me stand in for you while you sneak away and have the meeting?"

"What are you talking about, sweetie?"

"I could pretend to be you, Mom. Your body double. Truman had one. So did Kennedy. Why not you?"

Chapter Thirteen

"Because it'll never work," Mom said. "Truman and Kennedy didn't live under the same media scrutiny that we do. You don't even sound like me."

"Oh yeah? Hand me your cell phone."

"Come on, Morgan—"

"No, really. Let's put it to the test."

Mom shrugged and handed me her personal cell phone. I turned the volume up so Mom could hear the conversation, and hit the key to Dad's mobile. It only rang once before Dad's voice crackled through. "Everything all right, Sara?"

"Everything's fine," I said, careful to let my voice drop soothingly on the last syllable, like Mom would. "I just wanted to wish you a safe flight, and tell you I love you." I grimaced over this last bit.

A pause. Uh-oh. Maybe I wasn't as good at imitating Mom as I thought I was.

"Well, I love you, too, Sugarlips," Dad replied. I cringed. He called her Sugarlips? Gag. "When I get back, maybe I'll show you how much—"

I tried to cut him off before my ears were soiled any further. "That sounds fantastic—"

Mom, quivering with suppressed laughter, nudged me. She'd scribbled a word on a bubblegum wrapper and held it under my nose.

She can't be serious. "NO!" I mouthed to her.

"YES!" she mouthed back.

I made myself finish the sentence. "—Sweetcheeks."

Another pause. I really thought the jig was up, but then Dad murmured: "It's a date."

I said good-bye quickly before I learned any more about my parents' love life. No one needs to know that stuff. Ever.

"Sugarlips? Sweetcheeks? I think I'm gonna need therapy."

Mom let loose. I'd never seen her laugh so hard. "Sorry, sweetie," she said after she got a grip. "It's a code your father and I came up with, to let each other know that everything's okay."

"I think I threw up a little in my mouth."

"Try negotiating with the opposition party over environmental regulations. You'll get used to the taste of vomit." Mom's tone changed. "You may be able to pull off sounding like me, but looking like me? No way."

"Wanna bet?" I groped for my cell phone on my nightstand.

Three seconds later: "Hey, Hannah. Mom and I have a national emergency we need your help with." I explained that I needed her to bring her full makeup kit. "Can you come over right now?"

"And miss calculus? Hell, yeah! Mom'll write me a note if I tell her the president needs me. Be there in thirty."

She arrived in less than twenty, armed with her Louis Vuitton travel suitcase full of theater makeup, wigs, and prosthetics. "Max almost didn't let me up until they sonogrammed everything, but I told him the president was waiting. That boy is by the book."

"As he should be," Mom said, peering into the suitcase. "Oh my gosh, Hannah! What happened here?"

"Oh no!" Hannah pulled out a molten sack of plastic. "The security machine melted my supply of gel enhancers!"

Mom and I exchanged looks. Then we busted up again.

While Hannah dumped the bag of plastic goo in the trash, she asked, "So what's this national emergency?"

"I need you to make me look like my mom," I told her.

Hannah gave me and my mom a critical once-over. "Should be no problem. But the right costume is crucial. Seventy-five percent of the illusion is in the clothing."

"If I get one of her power suits on, no one will be able to tell us apart," I said.

"Make sure you stick to the sensible pumps," Hannah added, eyeing my bedhead. "And we'll have to make sure your hair is perfect. A wig should do it—"

"Hold up," Mom laughed. "You guys are really taking this seriously, aren't you?"

We stared at her. "Performance art is a serious business, Mrs. Abbott," Hannah said, well, seriously.

"Then we'd better go the whole way," Mom answered. "To the walk-in."

Mom and Dad's room had been redecorated by one of the foremost designers in Washington, D.C. Which meant it was as boring as a mustard-only hot dog. The soothing earth tones were already putting me to sleep. But one thing that did rule was Mom's amazing walk-in closet, complete with an automated clothing rack. Mom hit the button and hundreds of power suits whirred before us.

"Stop right there." Hannah hauled out three suits: one in red, one herringbone, and one bright blue. She held the red one up to me. "Hm. This shade of tomato is too strong for your coloring."

"Hey, that's my favorite suit!" Mom exclaimed.

"I've been meaning to tell you it was ready for the Salvation Army, Mrs. Abbott," Hannah replied. "With all due respect, it's all wrong for you. Stick to rosy red instead. It'll be much more flattering."

While Mom gazed sadly at her tomato-colored suit, her private phone line rang. It was to be the first call of many. Mom must've blown off Padma, Humberto, and a couple of aides about seventeen times before they got the hint and stopped calling. Or maybe it was Mom's crabby "I'll be downstairs when I'm downstairs" remark that finally got them off our backs.

While Mom took her belated shower, Hannah began the transformation. I slipped into the herringbone suit, which was a little snug in the shoulders and loose in the caboose, but nothing to worry about. Hannah applied a sensible swipe of taupe eye shadow and a light coating of mascara on my eyes. Instead of erasing dark circles, she created them and the illusion of a few slight creases around the eyes. Over my head, she carefully eased a wig that mimicked Mom's mahogany bob to perfection.

I stared at my reflection in Mom's three-paneled vanity mirror. "Holy cow."

Hannah gave herself a mock pat on the back. "Dum dum de dum," she sang, imitating the "Hail to the Chief" tune. "All rise for President Sara Abbott."

I really did look like my mother. The hair, the clothes. Even my clamped mouth (to keep me from screaming) echoed Mom when she was deep in thought. My reflection freaked me out a little.

Mom came out of the bathroom in a robe with her hair in a towel. "Oh. My. God," she said.

The swap was complete.

I rose from the vanity. "My fellow Americans," I intoned,

114

cocking my head slightly to the right just like Mom did during her State of the Unions. I pointed my index finger to the heavens. "Change comes from one person, and one person only: you."

I thought Mom's eyes were going to bug out of her head. "It's uncanny," she breathed.

I started pacing the room with Mom's rapid step. "Padma, take a memo," I said to Hannah, who leaped up and grabbed a pretend notebook. "Send it to all media outlets. Starting next week, my administration will propose that (a) white-chocolate gingersnaps will be the official White House cookie; (b) that anyone violating my newly proposed cookie accord with Oreos or Nutty Bars will be in breach of Executive Order Number 25768; and (c) that the recipe for white-chocolate gingersnaps be available on our website at no charge so that the American people can freely support this initiative."

Mom stepped forward and raised her hand. "Uh, Madam President, is it true that the white-chocolate gingersnap was in fact created by someone who is a British national? Therefore, isn't the White House's new cookie less than American both conceptually and in execution?"

I rubbed my ear just like Mom did when she was answering a tough question, and sidestepped it. "America is a melting pot of flavors. The white-chocolate gingersnap combines the sharp with the sweet—much like this fine nation. Our administration supports diversity and is committed to culinary equality."

"Nicely handled." Mom nodded approvingly. "But I don't rub my ear like that during press conferences."

Hannah and I exchanged looks and said, "Yes, you do!" in perfect unison.

There would be no convincing Mom unless she saw it with her own eyes, so I fired up her laptop and downloaded a YouTube clip of her latest press conference. Where she rubbed her ear about seven times in less than four minutes.

"Okay, okay. Point taken." Mom was biting her lip now. "I can't believe I'm even considering this."

"No gain without risk," I said. Another of Dad's mottos.

"If things weren't so dire in Africa, I'd never even contemplate it. I think I could clear my schedule so that you wouldn't be thrown into any dicey situations beyond a brief appearance, but even with the best laid plans, things could go wrong."

"I can handle it, Mom. It's just for a day, right?"

"And I can make sure no one will ever know the difference between you two," Hannah added.

Mom nibbled her lip again, then picked up her private line. For the first time ever, Mom called in sick. That's when I knew she was taking this plan seriously.

She asked Humberto to send up several files, and she spent the rest of the morning coaching me on the intricacies of the U.S. presidency.

Chapter Fourteen

Mom's private line chirped again.

"It's Humberto," she said with a glance at the LCD identification screen. "I think we're ready to test this plan out. If you can fool Humberto, you can fool anyone."

"Are we?" I took a bite of one of the Snickers bars Mom keeps stashed in her nightstand. The hairs on the bob-cut wig kept tickling the corner of my mouth, and somehow I got caramel on the fibers. At least Mom had let me put on some presidential sweats for the Humberto encounter.

Hannah, who'd been filing her nails since Mom started coaching me, examined her cuticles. "You were ready about an hour ago, Morgan. Relax, you got this down."

Mom picked up the phone. "Come on up," she told Humberto. "But keep your distance. I don't want you to get this bug I seem to have picked up."

A minute later, the Secret Service agent buzzed him up to

the residence wing.

Mom and Hannah headed to the walk-in closet when a knock rattled the bedroom door. "Get rid of the candy," Mom whispered. I chucked the half-eaten bar in the trash.

Hannah gave me a thumbs-up before sliding the closet door nearly shut.

Adrenaline shot through me. I could pull this off. I knew I could.

"Come in," I called. I picked up my mom's cell phone and held it to my ear as if I'd just taken a super important call. I kept my profile to Humberto when he entered.

"Thanks, Humberto. Just set the files on the nightstand, will you?" I'd gotten my mom's rapid-fire voice patterns down really well by now. I turned slightly away and spoke into the inactivated cell phone. "Sam, honey, we'll talk about it when you get back from London. Don't worry, I'll be sure to take my NyQuil and kick this bug."

I flipped the phone shut.

Humberto stood in the doorway, hands folded in front as was his custom. He raked my face with his eyes as if something puzzled him.

I kept my expression under control, but sweat started to bead under my wig. Maybe I wasn't as good at impersonating my mother as I thought.

Then he said: "I'm glad you listened to reason and

canceled the Africa trip, Sara."

Whew!

"Are you?" I judiciously sneezed and reached for a tissue.

Humberto took a tiny step back. "CENTCOM sent a briefing over from the Pentagon. The whole region's devolving into chaos. General Mfuso's ordered troops to the borders. The CIA thinks that war is about to break out. Not only are our strategic interests threatened, but famine is almost certainly guaranteed for the people of the Delta Valley, and there's no sign of the missing yellowcake. It's far too dangerous now—though I can't help but feel that having that meeting with Mfuso and Bishop Welak would have made all the difference."

"I know." I folded my arms and tapped the knuckle of my index finger over my pursed lips like Mom did when she was thinking hard. "This crisis is my highest priority today. There may be a way yet to solve it. Keep me informed of any updates."

"Will do."

"And could you keep the aides from bothering me with congressional requests today? I need to focus. Plus"—I sneezed again—"I don't want anyone else to catch this cold."

"You got it."

Humberto barely got the door shut behind him when Mom popped out of the closet. "I'm flabbergasted," she said.

"She fooled him, all right." Hannah emerged with one of

Mom's Hermès scarves twined around her throat. "Like there was any doubt."

Mom beamed and a warm feeling spread through me. I loved surprising my mom in a good way for once. "Piece of cake," I said modestly.

"I can't believe I'm saying this, but I think we can pull off a switch." Mom dug her handheld scheduling device out of the pocket of her robe and started rearranging things on the touchpad. "Maybe I'm crazy, but . . ."

"You're not crazy," I assured her. "This is the right thing to do."

Mom nodded. "I think a week is enough time to get Mfuso and Welak to the negotiating table, but I'll have to send in the CIA to guarantee their safety if we're to bring them to Camp David. . . ." Mom started to pace, muttering about Air Force 2, CENTCOM, high-level security, a media blackout, and the best way to break it to her chief of staff that her eighteen-year-old daughter just fooled him into thinking she was the president of the United States.

Meanwhile, Hannah gave my shoulder a squeeze. "You rock, President Morgan," she said.

"Frankly, I was skeptical," Mom interjected. "But you two proved me wrong." She smiled. "Hmm, after I finish briefing Humberto, I'll have to inform both your Secret Service detail and mine, of course."

"Tell Max?" My enthusiasm for the plan came to a screeching

halt. For some reason, the thought of Max seeing me in my mom's getup sent the heebie-jeebies through me. I could already hear him telling me the plan would never work.

"Do we have to?" I asked. "Maybe we should do another test run first."

"Good idea, sweetie." Mom beamed at me again like I was a rocket scientist. "I know what we can do. I'm supposed to host a reception for Prince Richard of Great Britain tonight. Why don't you stand in for me for a few minutes, just to test this out? If you can pull it off, we'll know for certain you can impersonate me successfully."

Hannah gasped. I mean, literally, audibly gasped. Which was weird, because normally Hannah was too cool to geek out over anything. "Prince Richard, *the* Prince Richard, is coming here? Tonight?"

"With his cute British accent," I teased. "And wavy black hair. One of Celebricity.com's one hundred and one most handsome hotties. *That* Prince Richard."

"Whoa, Morgan." Hannah picked up a copy of *Congressional Quarterly* and started fanning herself. "I hope you don't burst into flames standing next to him. Remember, you're supposed to be married to your dad."

"Now that's just gross, Hannah. You're letting the prince's hottitude fry your mind."

Mom started cracking up. "Oh, to be eighteen again," she

laughed. "I hope you can keep it together because if you can pull off this event, then maybe, just maybe, this crazy plan will work."

"Relax, Mom." My words were braver than I felt. "I can pull it off."

"I hope so, sweetie." Mom sobered up. "Because a lot of lives are on the line."

"I know."

Mom and I shared a look of understanding. We were Abbott women. We were strong. And together we could handle whatever the world chose to throw at us.

But what I couldn't handle was telling Max that I was impersonating my mother. I don't know why his opinion of me mattered so much, but it did.

In the end Mom was the one to tell him and she said he took the news like a professional. Sure, how else could he act? She was the commander in chief, after all. But I had no doubt that inside he was feeling the full force of another Tornado strike.

Chapter Fifteen

Luckily, the reception was to be a low-key affair at the prince's request. Just a few diplomats from the British embassy and the prince's entourage.

Hannah had to be home before dinner to attend an ACLU forum with her parents, so Mom picked out my clothes this time, insisting I wear her yellow St. John pantsuit for the reception. The one that made her—and now me—look like a stick of butter. I vowed then and there to toss any yellow items of clothing and dye my hair green when this was all over.

"It's conservative and appropriate for this occasion," Mom said while pinning an ugly jeweled lizard brooch, a gift from the queen, on the yellow lapel. She wore her robe so she'd be ready to quickly slip on the hideous pantsuit when I returned. "Don't forget to mention our initiative to raise international emissions standards to Prince Richard."

I giggled. "Sounds like you want me to talk about fart

suppression . . . maybe a ban on chili consumption in public places—"

"Would you be serious, Morgan?"

"Sorry." I cracked inappropriate jokes when I was nervous. Which, despite my big words of confidence, I was. Super nervous.

Mom's intercom system chirped.

"That means the guests are arriving," Mom said. She smoothed her hair. Then she smoothed mine. "I'll be watching everything from the security monitor. You're to spend fifteen minutes circulating and shaking hands. Then excuse yourself and have Special Agent Parker escort you back to the family wing. Humberto will cover while you and I swap back."

"Mom, we've gone over the plan a hundred times already!"

"I know. I know." She gave me an encouraging smile, which wobbled a little. "Showtime, sweetie. Good luck."

"Thanks." I took a deep breath before I opened her bedroom door. "Here goes."

I straightened my spine and hit the hallway leading out of the residence with my mother's trademark quick step. To my surprise, staff members either nodded at me or stood aside. Parker, the lead agent on Mom's Secret Service detail, waited for me at the elevator that would take me from the third-floor residence to the second floor where the reception was to be held. He didn't even bat an eye.

So far, so good. The plan was going off without a hitch.

Already, guests were filing into the Yellow Oval Room, which is where Mom liked to hold private receptions for important dignitaries. Now I got it. Yellow pantsuit to match the yellow Louis XVI decor.

Good thing Mom was a gifted politician. Because her fashion sense needed help.

Humberto approached. Nervously, I smoothed the front of the suit.

"Feeling better, *President Abbott*?" he inquired ironically.

I'll say this for Humberto. Mom chose him well, because earlier today he met the news that I was impersonating my mother so she could broker a secret peace deal between two warring African juntas with barely a ripple of emotion. Either he thought it was a good idea or Humberto was really good at hiding an internal freak-out.

Smart money on the latter.

I cleared my throat. "Where's the prince?"

"On the balcony. He's impressed with the view."

Of course. The view from the Truman Balcony happened to be the best in Washington, D.C. In the setting sun, the Washington Monument glowed pink and gold, while lights from jets landing at Reagan International Airport twinkled like stars in the twilit sky. A pond with a lighted fountain added a splash of color on the swath of green lawn rolling toward Capitol Hill.

Humberto took my elbow and whispered, "Morgan, are you sure you can do this?"

"Yes." *Stop asking questions, Humberto!* He was starting to flip me out. "I mustn't keep the prince waiting any longer. Mom, I mean, *I* wouldn't approve."

I plunged into the gathering and headed straight to the balcony. I'd shake hands later, but for now I deftly weaved and dodged the ambassador to the United Kingdom and her husband and a couple of embassy diplomats. Parker stationed himself by the doorway, ready to intervene in case things went awry. I almost missed Max's disapproving frown, but it would be a dead giveaway to have him shadowing me at the reception instead of Mom's agent.

Let me state for the record that Prince Richard looks nothing like the photos I've seen of him in the celebrity mags. He's much, much hotter. No wonder Hannah freaked out . . . the next king of England should have been modeling underwear on a billboard in Times Square.

Too bad he seemed bored out of his skull.

Prince Richard's famous sapphire eyes were glazed over with a dull stare of polite interest as he spoke to one of the dignitaries. It was an expression I'd worn a bajillion times at these types of functions.

I greeted the prince with what I hoped was motherly presidential interest. "And how has your visit been progressing?"

I asked after we'd worn out the usual pleasantries about airplane travel and the weather.

"It's been smashing," he said in his chippy British accent. "The ribbon cutting at the new U.K./U.S. appliance-manufacturing factory in Utica was quite enthralling, as was the North Atlantic Fisheries conference in Bangor. Lovely places, Bangor and Utica."

"Really?"

"Indeed. I feel as though our two countries are close on an accord regarding, erm, cod and haddock quotas."

"Excellent." God, how did Mom keep from passing out with boredom? And poor Prince Richard looked as if his brain was atrophying before my eyes.

I opened my mouth to discuss the international emissions standards Mom insisted I mention, and found myself saying: "Would you like to have some fun?"

Prince Richard choked on a sip of spring water. "Pardon?"

I repeated myself. "My daughter, Morgan, is about your age—perhaps you two could hang out and have some fun." I gave him what I hoped was a motherly wink. "It's a little boring around here, isn't it?"

Prince Richard took a moment to politely consider the offer, but he couldn't conceal the relief rippling over his face. "I'd be delighted to meet your daughter, Madam President."

"Excellent." Suddenly I realized Humberto was at my elbow.

He shot me a meaningful look. My fifteen minutes as leader of the free world was up. "Would you excuse me for a moment, Your Highness? I need to make a few arrangements."

"Of course." Prince Richard gave the cutest formal bow, totally Old World European.

Parker appeared at my other elbow.

These guys didn't mess around. Before I knew it, I'd been whisked away back upstairs to my parents' room, where my mother waited anxiously.

"Well? How'd it go?" she asked as I handed over the suit. "It looked successful from what I could see on the security feed."

"Pretty good. No one gave me funny looks at all. Oh, by the way, I made a date tonight. With Prince Richard."

Mom shrugged into her pantsuit jacket. "You work fast. Konner who?"

I laughed and handed Mom her sensible pumps. "It's not like that. I feel sorry for the guy. He had to attend a conference on fishing *and* appliance manufacturing."

"Purgatory," Mom agreed. "Just keep the fun low-key, Morgan. Okay?"

"Sure, Mom. We'll play pinochle in the Treaty Room or croquet on the North Lawn."

"I was thinking you two could go bowling in the White House bowling alley."

"Uh . . . I'll ask him." Bowling? Yeah, right.

I gave my mom a kiss on the cheek. "See you in the morning."

Once in my room I tore off the wig and ran my fingers over my itchy scalp. I scrubbed my face and added a swipe of daring lip color. A squirt of hairspray fluffed up my flattened hair. Once I slipped into jeans and a funky top, I felt like myself again.

Parker called the family line to tell me the Secret Service detail had moved Prince Richard to the Treaty Room, which was next door to the Yellow Oval Room. When I arrived, Prince Richard was peering out of the south-facing window, where night now lay velvety over the spectacular Washington, D.C., skyline.

"Hey there." I stuck out my hand and introduced myself.

The prince took it gratefully.

"Ready to get out of here?" I asked him.

"Absolutely!" The prince's gorgeous eyes shifted to his cadre of aides hovering at a discreet distance. "But where would we go?"

"I've got a few ideas. There's just one important thing I have to deal with before we can go."

The prince sighed. "Security."

"Bingo."

He gestured to a nearby member of his staff. "That will give me time to ask someone to go to my suite at the Watergate and get me some appropriate clothes."

"Great! See you in a bit."

I excused myself and went to find Max. He wasn't at all happy when I informed him that I wanted to go out with Prince Richard, the most photographed celebrity in the world.

"C'mon, Max," I wheedled. "The poor guy's been stuck at official functions since he came to the U.S. Besides, my mom wants me to entertain him."

"Was this you as your mom or the real president?"

"It was my idea, but Mom agreed."

Max's jaw hardened and I could see the vein on his neck pulse above his buttoned-up collar. "And what do you think she meant by the word 'entertain'?" he asked sharply.

I blinked. Was Max angry at me? "She'd love it if we played Scrabble and drank lemonade, but since it's a Friday night, I was thinking of something more exciting . . . like dancing."

"Morgan—"

"What if we go to the Purple Panda? They've got a new DJ."

"Out of the question. For one thing, you're underage."

"How about Asylum, then? They always book killer bands." The more Max resisted my plan, the more I wanted to do it.

Max ran a hand through his short-cropped hair in frustration. "May I remind you that you're still a minor?"

"Please, so are you! It's not like no one ever snuck into a nightclub before they reached legal drinking age. Besides, we're not going out to drink, we're going out to dance."

"Morgan. I'm serious. The security of both you and the prince is too important to compromise for a night out on the town."

"Max. I'm serious, too. Prince Richard and I want out of The Bubble for a little while. I'll call Hannah, too. She's got a huge crush on the guy . . . it'll be an early birthday present for her."

"You want Hannah to come?"

"Sure. Plus you'll be there, as will the prince's detail. What could go wrong?"

Max chewed his lip. At the mention of Hannah, the tension around his shoulders seemed to ease. "All right," he said after a long moment of consideration. "But we do this my way. I'll call in a favor, and see if we can get you into Vex."

"Vex?" Holy cow! Vex was the hottest club in the metro D.C. area!

"I know the head of security there," Max continued. "I'll send the advance team to sweep the place. I'll check if the VIP room is available, too."

I gave a yelp of joy.

"BUT—and Morgan, this is a big but—you've got to promise me not to do anything crazy."

"I promise to remain in visual contact with my Secret Service team at all times." I crossed my heart.

"If I say we have to move out, we have to move out. No lip, no flack."

"Got it."

"Why do I get the feeling I'm going to regret this?" Max muttered.

"Nah." I punched him playfully on the arm. "Nothing's going to go wrong. You're in charge, remember?"

Max regarded me warily. Or was that wearily? "Being in charge of a tornado is much harder than it looks," he said.

Chapter Sixteen

"Secret Agent Man is getting us into Vex? With Prince Richard?" Hannah squealed. "No way!"

"He knows a guy."

"Impressive."

It was. It really was. Max went up a notch or two in my estimation, but nothing could prepare me for the sight of Max when Prince Richard and I arrived at the motorpool. My baby-faced Secret Service agent was dressed in a black shirt—no tie in sight—and well-worn jeans slung low at his hips to show off flat abs. Had that hot bod been lurking under his boring gray business suit all this time?

"Who's that bloke?" Prince Richard asked. He'd changed into an exquisitely tailored Euro-style shirt topped with a leather bomber jacket and knitted skullcap that covered his distinctive wavy black hair.

"That's my Secret Service agent." I blinked a couple times to make sure. Max looked almost . . . cool.

"What's the deal?" I asked Max, who stood by the door of the limo, waiting. "Where's the suit?"

Despite the new clothes, Max was all business. "I have to blend in, Morgan. Unless you want everyone in Vex to know that the president's daughter and Prince Richard of Great Britain are getting their groove on with them."

True. Max would stick out like a sore thumb in his business suit.

Still. It unnerved me how different he looked—like he should be sitting next to me in calculus class instead of muttering into his wireless com and concealing his government-issue firearm.

I tried to ignore Max as the limo slid through traffic to the revitalized part of Anacostia's waterfront, where Hannah's parents owned one of the new high-rises going up near the Nationals' baseball stadium. Lights glittered over the Anacostia River, and good hostess that I was, I pointed out notable landmarks to the prince like the Marvin Gaye Memorial Park and the historic wharves, which the British burned down in 1812.

The prince, good guest that he was, feigned polite interest and apologized for the burnings until Hannah emerged from the lobby of the luxury condo; then he became Scooby-Doo eyeing a Scooby Snack. Hannah had pulled out all the stops for this occasion. A clingy knit dress in a gorgeous shade of fuchsia set off her chocolate skin, and she'd straightened her hair so it flowed silkily over her shoulders. The gold choker around her throat and matching armband bracelet winked in the light of the street lamp.

Gracefully she folded herself into the limo. "Lovely to meet you, Prince Richard," she said in a low sultry voice, and held her hand out to him.

The prince swallowed, then hastily took her outstretched hand. "And you," he murmured.

Max and I exchanged glances. Poor guy didn't stand a chance.

A massive line snaked from the front door of Vex to around the block, but the advance team had managed to clear the back entrance for us. The Secret Service also posted agents in strategic places around the club's interior.

Max checked me before we headed in. "Remember your promise, Morgan." The expression on his face was tense.

I knew the hardest security situations were in public places like this. That's why the Secret Service tried to keep people like the prince and me contained inside The Bubble, where they could control conditions.

"Nothing crazy's going to happen. Just fun tonight," I assured him.

But Max didn't look reassured at all. "This place is sick!" Hannah yelled into my ear over the pulsing music.

"Isn't it awesome?" I screeched back. Friday night and Vex

was packed. Lasers shot blades of light over the wall-to-wall patrons. A DJ wearing shredded urban wear and a Nationals baseball cap stood on a lit platform and mixed dance cuts.

Hannah immediately pulled an unresisting Prince Richard onto the dance floor. They melded pretty well into the crowd heaving to a hip-hop remix of disco tunes. Smoke from dry-ice machines misted the room, and a disco ball lowered from the ceiling.

The whole thing—the music, the special effects—was so killer, the urge to dance overwhelmed me. No wonder Vex earned a reputation as the hottest club in D.C. I scanned the room looking for someone who would dance with me. But the only people nearby were security agents from the prince's detail, and Max.

Desperate times . . .

"Come on, Max!" I pulled at his arm. "Let's dance."

He jerked away so hard, he elbowed one of the prince's MI5 agents in the ribs. "That's not a good idea, Morgan. I need to stay alert."

"But it'll look less suspicious. See, people are already starting to wonder about you guys."

Max cast a hunted look at the cocktail tables over by the bar. Sure enough, some people were nodding and turning in my direction.

"Well . . . I guess it makes sense. . . ."

A remixed Madonna song pumped through the sound system. That did it. I didn't wait for Max to finish his sentence. I hauled him out on the dance floor and began grooving.

Max stood before me, eyes wide with shock, watching me gyrate. I may be the president's daughter but I've got some moves.

"Get it together." I laughed. "Dance!"

Max moved robotically for a few beats, and the thought crossed my mind that maybe I should have gone it alone. If the floor were any less crowded, Max would have been a little embarrassing. Then all at once he relaxed and his movements became fluid.

I flashed him a grin.

Max jerked his shoulders in a cool b-boy bodywave, and once again I realized that there was more to Special Agent Max Jackson than I'd previously suspected.

With Hannah and Prince Richard next to us, we danced through three decades of remixed hits. The floor became even more crowded, and heat from dancing bodies steamed up the wall mirrors.

We were pushed into the center of the packed dance floor. I couldn't see anything over the heads of the bobbing dancers. My T-back halter top stuck between my shoulder blades, and the hair on the nape of my neck curled in the humidity.

The remix of nineties house music ended in a staccato drum

solo. Then a slow song tinkled over the sound system.

I expected the floor to empty so I could grab a drink of mineral water, but no such luck. More dancers flooded on. We were stuck.

I saw Hannah and the prince sink into each other. She gave me a big fat wink over Prince Richard's shoulder and settled her head on his shoulder.

I glanced at Max. Sweat plastered his short brown hair into spikes and I could see him looking for a way out of the packed floor.

I tried teasing him even though I felt a little weird myself. "You said you'd take a bullet for me. One slow dance won't kill you."

"Remember that this is in the line of duty," he quipped, but the smile didn't quite reach his eyes. He pulled me close; I draped my arms across his shoulders and we shuffled. I smelled his aftershave and tried not to think about how solid his biceps felt around me. Or the holster of his sidearm digging into my side.

Max tilted his head against mine. And then I tried not to think about how much I liked *that*. For a moment, I forgot that he'd been hired to do a job—protect me. Instead, all I could think about is how right it felt to be in his arms.

I sighed and snuggled closer; he tightened his hold on me.

Then he stiffened.

"What is it?" I asked.

"Cell phone video recorder," he murmured into my ear. "Our cover's been blown. We have to move."

By the time Max had cleared a path to the door, the energy in the club had changed. Now a familiar buzz hummed underneath the music, and people were nudging one another and trying to get snaps of the prince and me on their cell phone cameras.

The security detail closed in. Max ushered us through the kitchen while he arranged for the Baby Beast to meet us at the back door. Unfortunately, a bunch of photographers and videographers already packed the alley hoping for that million-dollar shot.

"Your Royal Highness," Max said to Prince Richard, "I'm afraid the paparazzi have discovered you."

"Ah well." Prince Richard slipped his arm around Hannah's waist. "It was entirely worth it."

The flash of cameras and digital recorders nearly blinded us. I grabbed Prince Richard's hand to keep him from being mauled by a group of screaming girls and yanked him into the Baby Beast. Hannah and Max flung themselves in after us, and we rolled.

Max and I politely stared out opposite windows as the D.C. skyline eased by, while Hannah and the prince snuggled close. I reached for a bottle of water in the limo's wet bar and my hand accidentally grazed Max's. An electric shock passed between us. He jerked away like he'd been burned.

Whoa.

Was I beginning to fall for my Secret Service agent?

Chapter Seventeen

"I told you to keep the fun low-key, Morgan."

Mom slapped the front page of *The Washington Post* next to my bowl of Frosted Flakes. She and I were eating breakfast in the family kitchenette.

With a sinking feeling, I stared at the grainy photo of me and Prince Richard ducking out of Vex's back door. I was holding Prince Richard's hand, and he happened to have his head turned toward me so that his gorgeous profile was perfectly captured. Max and Hannah were nowhere to be seen. Probably Photoshopped out of the shot.

"Mom, I can explain." My mind raced. I didn't want to get Max in trouble.

"You know what?" Mom sighed. She looked unusually tired. "I honestly don't want to know. You and the prince made it home safely, and that's the main thing."

Mom's taking a pass on giving me a lecture? *My* mother?

"Is everything okay?"

"Actually, it is." Mom took a sip of her herbal green tea and spread soy butter on her sprouted wheat toast. "I made real progress with the Mfuso junta last night. I think he might be ready to play ball after all."

"That's excellent, Mom!"

Mom allowed herself to crack a smile. "It *is* pretty excellent, isn't it? But this means that next Saturday, you'll have to be me again while I hold the meeting. Are you sure, Morgan? Totally, one hundred percent sure you can do this?"

I waved my spoon airily over my bowl of Frosted Flakes. "If you can get warring African military juntas to agree to a cease-fire and save the world from nuclear destruction, then I can pose as the president of the United States for a day."

She reached for my hand, her expression stone-cold serious. "If we're caught in this deception, it'll mean the end of my presidency. I could be impeached. You could . . . I don't want to even entertain that thought. . . ."

I swallowed hard. I'd thought about the consequences already. "We have to do something, don't we?" I squeezed her hand. "Look on the bright side: I'd have more time to study in jail."

Mom and I exchanged grins across the table, hers more reluctant than mine.

For the rest of the weekend, I tried not to think about our

swap, yellowcake uranium, or Konner. Mom and I did the usual rounds of honoring Earth Day volunteers and a couple of Olympic athletes. I managed to catch up on some homework and a sense of normal seeped in—well, as normal as my life gets. It was a relief after the week I'd had.

But Monday morning, once again, whispers followed me through the halls of the Academy of the Potomac. Copies of the *Washington Post's* gossip page, the *Gadfly*, and even downloaded photos of Celebricity.com's website littered the cafeteria and library. The press was going crazy speculating about President Abbott's wayward daughter and Prince Richard. Max didn't bother to confiscate the papers. There were too many.

Even Hannah was annoyed. "They make it look like you and Rich are an item," she said as we hoisted our massive chemistry books out of our lockers for class.

I raised a brow. "Rich?"

"Yeah. He called." Hannah casually checked the text messages on her cell phone. Then she showed me the log of incoming calls.

RICH

RICH

RICH

I cracked up. Leave it to Hannah. If anyone could snag the world's most eligible bachelor, it'd be her.

"And guess who else thinks you two are an item?" Hannah

tilted her head to the left.

Konner Tippington hung around his locker and pretended to play with the texting pad on his cell phone, but it was so obvious he was faking. He gave me a nod and one of his charming grins, which would have sent me running right over to him in the past.

Not this time.

"The boy is mad jealous," Hannah added with a laugh. "Jeong told me that Konner punched his gym locker when he saw the photo."

"He did?" I had to admit that was satisfying even though I wasn't missing Konner the way I thought I would. Sure, he was scorching hot. Super popular. And could be charming when he wanted to be. But I never felt butterflies doing the cha-cha in my stomach the way I did when I danced with Max at the club.

While I mulled that fact over I must have been gazing at Konner. Apparently, he took it for encouragement, because he started to walk over.

Involuntarily I scooted closer to Max, who'd been waiting for me out of earshot and was politely examining a homecoming dance poster while Hannah and I finished gossiping. Max was wearing jeans and a graphic tee today, which, he explained, enabled him to blend better with his surroundings. Now, despite his earpiece, with his short-cropped hair and clean-shaven chin, he seemed more like a captain of the lacrosse team, or maybe an ace member of the tech club, than a trained Secret Service agent.

Max looked up and saw Konner heading our way. His eyes went a smidge colder. "Ready for class, Morgan?"

"So ready."

Hannah and I turned our shoulders on Konner; Max took up the rear, effectively freezing Konner out.

"Nice," Hannah whispered as we headed to the chem lab. "Secret Agent Man comes in handy sometimes, doesn't he? Like at the club the other night?" She shot me a sly look. "I think he likes you."

"Max? No way. There're all sorts of rules against agents getting friendly with protectees." But I couldn't help feeling a zing of hope. Maybe my imagination wasn't playing tricks on me after all.

I gave Max a grateful smile when we reached the lab, and he nodded back.

For the rest of the day, Max played keep-away between Konner and me, and the funniest part of the whole thing was that I don't think Konner had a clue. One minute I'd be right in front of him, the next minute Max would whisk me away, leaving Konner swimming in confusion.

Konner aside, and despite the whispers and gossip about my picture in the paper, the day meandered on uneventfully. Until Ms. Gibson appeared before me in the hall right before calculus class.

"Morgan, I'd like to see you in my office, please."

I cast a hunted look at Max, but this time he just shrugged. Obviously, he knew better than to get between me and Tomb-Raider Gibson.

Once I settled into my all-too-familiar place on the other side of her desk, Gibson pushed a copy of the *New York Post*'s Page Six gossip column toward me. The pixilated image of my face showed me blinking like a doofus, while Prince Richard appeared to be looking down my shirt.

"What's the deal with this, Morgan? I believe this photo was taken Friday night, the same day you called in sick from school."

Crud. "Well, uh . . ."

"Did you seriously cut school? With grades like yours?"

God, Gibson looked so scary right now. I think I should recommend her to my mom for the position of head terrorism czar. Her interrogation methods would turn any terrorist into a quivering mass of Jell-O.

"It's not like that, Ms. Gibson, really it isn't. I, uh . . ." My mind kicked into warp speed. It's not like I could tell her that I had spent the day learning how to impersonate the president of the United States.

"I was, uh, sick in the morning, but then I got better." I winced. How lame did *that* sound?

146

"Got better." Ms. Gibson's voice dripped with contempt. "Yes, I can certainly see how going to a nightclub would be conducive to your health. Whether it contributes to your intellectual health is another matter entirely."

I opened my mouth to tell her that some things were more important than school. Like helping my mom prevent nuclear proliferation.

But I couldn't blow Mom's plans just to avoid another demerit in my file. "It won't happen again, Ms. Gibson. Clubbing with Prince Richard was a one-shot deal. You can be sure of that."

"And skipping school?"

"Never again." *If I could help it,* I added silently.

Ms. Gibson seared me with one of her penetrating glares. "I'm going to hold you to that, Morgan. Now get to class."

I booked out of there.

Just outside of Gibson's office, I spotted Brittany Whittaker and her posse cooing over a huge bouquet of flowers. Today Brittany wore a powder-blue mini and strappy sandals that made her legs look obscenely long and lean.

My feet in their scuffed Converse high-tops automatically turned in the opposite direction, but Brittany's honeydew voice curled around me. "Hey there, Morgan! Visiting Ms. Gibson again? I hope you're not going on academic probation this semester."

Brittany's minions tittered on cue.

Since I could never be certain academic probation wasn't in my future, I quickly changed the subject. "What's with the flowers? Laying them on the grave of some other person's stolen dreams?"

Brittany smirked. "We're consulting with Mrs. Hsu on appropriate decorations for the homecoming dance. Our committee is kicking it up a notch this year . . . last year's crepe paper and homemade posters were super tacky."

Ouch. I'd headed up the decorating committee for last year's homecoming dance.

"And I'm really sorry to hear about you and Konner breaking up. Such a shame. The two of you made a . . . an interesting couple."

I was about to tell her I'd remember that the next time I went clubbing with Prince Richard, the most scorching of the British royals, when my nose tingled and I let out a great big woof of a sneeze.

The posse jumped back.

"Ew, gross!" one of them yelped.

I sneezed again. And again.

"God, get her a tissue," Brittany snapped.

I scrubbed my nose with the offered Kleenex. "I'm allergic to lilies," I muttered. "It runs in the family."

"I thought white lilies were the president's favorite flower," she sneered.

"It's my dad who's allergic." Another sneeze exploded out of my nose. "I gotta get out of here."

As I walked rapidly away, I heard Brittany say, "Let's double the order of lilies for the dance."

Brittany Whittaker's evilness should have ticked me off, but since I didn't have a date for the homecoming dance anyway, I didn't really care. If she wanted to blow the senior class's social fund on expensive flowers that would end up like brown potpourri, let her deal with the fallout from the student council treasurer.

It wasn't like the school elected me class president. Besides, I had my own problems to cope with. Like running the country on Saturday.

Chapter Eighteen

"How'd it go with the guidance counselor?" Max asked as he held the door to the Baby Beast open for me. We'd walked to where the perimeter detail waited with the motorcade outside AOP's gates.

"Okay, I guess. I mean, I'm not expelled . . . yet."

I was about to sling my loaded backpack into the limo when Max took it and hefted it inside for me.

Agents *never* do personal chores like that. Ever. It's against the regulations, meant to keep them from becoming personal servants.

Max slipped in next to me and my heart accelerated.

The limo slid through light midafternoon traffic until we hit the predictable gridlock on the Taft Bridge. I stared at one of the enormous stone lions that guarded the entry onto the bridge.

"You're quiet today," Max remarked. "Are you sure everything's all right?"

After being slammed by Ms. Gibson and Brittany, I was overwhelmed by Max's kindness. I nodded. "Thanks, Max." I leaned over and nudged him with my shoulder.

"For what?"

"It's just nice, you know, having you around." I smiled.

Now Max looked really uncomfortable.

He scooted closer to the window and sighed. "Morgan, I think I may have given you the wrong idea."

"What?" I frowned. I thought we were having a moment.

"I think I may have gotten a little too"—he paused—"comfortable with you."

"What are you talking about?"

"There are rules against fraternization between agents and protectees." He wouldn't even look at me.

"What do you mean 'fraternization'?" OMG, did he think I was coming on to him? "I thought we were friends."

"I'm your Secret Service agent and you are my protectee." Max swallowed hard as if it were difficult to say. "That's all."

"You don't have to read me the Secret Service manual," I said dully. "I get it."

"There are reasons why rules and regulations exist," he continued doggedly. "They help prevent mistakes."

"Mistakes."

"Yeah. Mistakes. Ones that could cost you your life."

My head knew that Max was right. But my heart felt like

he'd stomped all over it. I turned my face away and stared out the window, but the D.C. scenery had somehow lost its luster.

We didn't speak for the rest of the ride home.

By Wednesday, I could tell Konner was getting desperate to talk to me. For the past two days I'd ignored his text messages and phone calls and didn't look at him during drama rehearsal, which I spent coaching my understudy in the role of Maureen. I made it a point to sit with Hannah at lunch, and pointedly moved if Konner tried to sit next to me.

Even though I was getting him back for dumping me, the effort was beginning to wear me down. I didn't like being mean.

So when Konner got behind me in the cafeteria line, I didn't drop out of the queue like I would have the day before. I decided to try a new tactic: ignoring him.

"Hey, Morgan, wassup?" he asked. Like nothing had ever happened.

Ignore.

"You look smokin' today, babe."

I was wearing a faded T-shirt and a pair of baggy jeans. Nice try.

He grabbed a sports drink and nervously shook it. "I, uh, wanted to tell you something."

That's when I got reeeeally interested in the mac 'n' cheese the lunch lady was doling out.

"Jeez, Morgan, would you at least look at me?"

I took a fruit cup and a bag of Cheetos and *No,* I thought, *I won't look at you, Konner Tippington, because I know you'll be zapping me with your melting blue eyes. Those gorgeous, gorgeous eyes.*

I picked up my tray and headed into the lunchroom to find Hannah. Fred, one of the perimeter team agents, was on lunch duty today because Max had to take an important call. To be honest, I was kind of relieved that he wasn't here. Neither of us could relax when the other was around lately and Max had gone back to doing things scrupulously by the book. Robo-agent Max Jackson was back.

Fred stood out like a sore thumb in his business suit, but at least he kept his distance. Unfortunately, I couldn't see Hannah, so I found a vacant spot near a window and sat down.

Quicker than Usain Bolt, Konner slipped into the chair next to me.

"Surprise!" Konner grinned cheesily at me.

I rose, but he grabbed my wrist.

"C'mon, Morgan. Don't bail. I've been trying to talk to you all week."

"I thought by now you'd get that I don't want to talk to you."

"I don't blame you, Morgan. Honestly."

Wha . . . ?

Konner wore an uncharacteristically humble expression. "Could you just hear me out? If you don't like what I'm saying, feel free to blow me off for the rest of our lives."

The sincerity in his voice really got to me. I sat down. "Okay. You've got one minute."

He nodded seriously. "I was an ass to you that night at the sushi bar. But I freaked. The media frenzy, the Secret Service detail, I couldn't handle it. To top it off, you looked so beautiful that night, I honestly couldn't believe that the president's daughter wanted to date a guy like me. I know I come on a little strong sometimes—"

"A little?"

"Okay, a lot. But I've learned my lesson."

Despite my effort to remain skeptical, he got me listening, spellbound. Me, beautiful? Me, freaking Konner Tippington out?

"I really miss you, Morgan." He hung his head like the admission cost him something. "Could we get back together?"

I automatically started shaking my head. Put my heart through the Konner Tippington meat grinder again? No way.

But out of the corner of my eye, I caught sight of Max returning to his station by the door. His eyes zeroed in on me talking to Konner. I was suddenly reminded of how stupid I'd been to think someone like Max would fall for someone like me.

We were all business and that was that.

Konner continued, a touch of desperation in his voice. "At least let me take you to the homecoming dance on Saturday—"

I glanced at Max and felt a tug of sadness. "Okay."

"—because I really want to make everything up to you—"

"I said okay, Konner. You can take me to the dance."

"I can?" He perked up.

Max's full attention locked on us now. I made a big show of leaning over to Konner and wrapping my arms around his shoulders. "We'll have a great time," I said, smiling like mad into his face.

Konner reacted like lightning. He planted an intense kiss on me and practically sucked my lips off.

When I got over my surprise, I pulled away.

And stared right up at Max looming over us.

"Class starts soon, Morgan," Max said tonelessly.

Konner tightened his grip on my waist. "Relax, dude. We've got time for this."

Konner lowered his head to mine again. I gave him a halfhearted kiss back and pulled away quickly. Max had moved to wait for me under the lighted exit sign, but I felt confused and embarrassed. As if I'd disappointed him.

"I got reamed again by Gibson," I told Konner. "So I'd better not be late for any more classes."

Konner resisted when I pulled away from him, but the

explanation made him relax. "Okay. I'll text you later."

"Yeah. Later."

Max followed me down the halls without a word.

I met Hannah by our locker. "Guess what? Konner's taking me to the homecoming dance."

"Konner?" She made a gagging noise. "Are you two back together?"

"I wouldn't say that. But I'm letting him take me to the dance. It's a test to see if he can stop acting like a jerk for one night. Besides, it's not like anyone else is going to ask me." I couldn't help glancing at Max waiting nearby.

"Hold up," Hannah muttered. "Aren't you supposed to be the president on Saturday?"

"Uh . . ."

Leave it to me to forget something as monumental as me impersonating the president of the United States.

"I can do both," I said with a confidence I only partially felt. "President by day, hot disco mama by night. Piece of cake."

Hannah wasn't fooled by my bull. "You're pushing your luck, girl."

Didn't I know it.

But now I had a new mission: score a killer dress for the homecoming dance. Hannah bagged out of shopping with me because she was seeing Prince Richard off on his private jet. So I instructed Max to send the advance team to my favorite boutique in Union Station. I told myself the hot dress was because I wanted Brittany Whittaker to drop dead with envy. And if I left a certain Secret Service agent nursing his regrets, so much the better.

Union Station had to be about my favorite place in D.C. Part shopping mall, part historical museum, and all gorgeous Art Deco architecture. I'll never forget Mom's inauguration ball held smack in the middle of the train station. The cavernous interior had been packed shoulder to shoulder with black-tie guests. Stars and stripes everywhere. The "President's Own" United States Marine Marching Band played "Hail to the Chief" for Mom the first time that night, and I remembered how my heart swelled with pride to see my mom stride across the stage and be welcomed as the president of the United States.

I grabbed a box of chicken nuggets at the food court and headed toward Mimi's Boutique with Max on my heels. He'd had the advance team sweep the store, so Mimi herself was waiting for me when I arrived.

"Morgan, honey, it's been too long." Mimi swept me up in a big hug, her dreadlocks bouncing and million bracelets jangling. "Big date coming up?"

"Yeah. Can you hook me up with something sick?"

"Have-His-Tongue-Hanging-Out sick, or She's-Gonna-Die-With-Envy sick?"

"How about both?" I needed a miracle—a dress to make

157

Konner humble, Brittany jealous, and Max forget the rule book.

"You got it." Mimi sorted through her amazing inventory of funky-chic dresses and loaded a dressing room with options.

I slipped a silk mini dyed in an intense shade of violet over my head and regarded my reflection critically. Hmm. I wasn't wild about the asymmetrical hemline. I wished Hannah were here to help me with this decision.

I swept the dressing room curtain aside. Maybe Mimi could give me an unbiased opinion.

Mimi was nowhere to be seen. But Max stood by a rack of beaded camis next to the full-length mirror, clearly bored out of his mind.

"Max." I strutted toward him like a supermodel on a runway. I struck a pose, then spun slowly. "What do you think?"

Max's brows snapped up. "It's, erm, an interesting look," he said carefully.

No help. What did guys know about fashion, anyway?

Back in the dressing room, I gave the dress another once-over.

Oh. My. God.

What I took to be an asymmetrical hemline was in actuality the back of the dress stuck in my neon green boy-briefs. Which Max just saw up close and personal.

I let out a shriek of horror.

"What is it?" In a flash, Max was right outside the dressing room. "Is something wrong?"

Nothing that being swallowed up by the floor wouldn't take care of.

"I'm coming in there if you don't answer me," he persisted.

"Don't!" My face flamed. "The last thing I need is my Secret Service agent seeing my underwear *again*."

Silence.

Then a splutter of laughter.

I yanked the curtain aside. Max stood there shaking with suppressed laughter.

"It's not funny," I said sourly.

"Actually, it was." A big fat grin split his face. God, he was so cute when he laughed like that. "Knowing you prefer boy shorts could be crucial information for your file."

"Don't you dare!" I threw my wadded-up T-shirt at him. "If this incident makes it into my file, I'll have my mom put you on the Caboodles detail."

Caboodles was the previous president's cocker spaniel, much beloved by the American people and hated by White House staffers for its evil temper and incontinence.

Max cracked up again. "C'mon, Morgan, you know me better than that," he said when he got himself under control. "Besides, I think your underwear preference is already in your file."

"Max!" I wailed.

"Sorry. Bad joke." He became contrite when he saw how upset I remained. "Don't worry, Morgan. This is between us. A Secret Service agent takes his protectees' secrets to the grave."

"You better. Or I'll make sure your grave is an early one." But I gave a reluctant grin of relief.

The cell phone in Max's jeans pocket chirped and he was all business again.

"Excuse me," he said, and turned away to take the call. I disappeared back inside the dressing room, and had tried on a cherry-colored halter dress when I heard him say: "I'll be there as soon as possible."

His tone made my heart stop beating. Something serious had happened.

I stuck my head around the curtain. "What is it?"

Max had been staring blindly at the cell phone in his hand, face white. "It's my mother. She's been in an accident."

Chapter Nineteen

"Oh my god!" I ran over to him. "You've got to go be with her, Max."

"Yeah." Dazed, he pulled his wireless com out from the pocket of his shirt. "I need to call in a replacement agent."

"Don't be silly, we can't wait for a backup. Let's go! We'll use the limo. We can cut through traffic if we put on the lights and siren."

"I can't do that. It's the property of the president—"

"Max!"

I shook his shoulders. "The president's daughter wants to go to where your mother is right now and that's an order."

"Yeah. Okay. Thanks, Morgan."

Ten minutes later we were in the car. Max directed the driver to head to the northeast area of D.C. Glitzy shops and condos were replaced by dilapidated apartment buildings and dollar stores. Graffiti. Plastic sacks of uncollected garbage piled on corners.

We pulled up outside a run-down brick building that looked like it'd once been an office suite. NORTHSIDE HOMELESS ADVOCACY CENTER was painted over the scarred door. A line of shabbily dressed people, some with kids, waited patiently on the sidewalk. A CLOSED sign hung crookedly out front.

A homeless shelter?

"You wait here," Max ordered. "I'll be right back."

Yeah, right. I waited a second and then scrambled after him.

The cavernous interior of the building looked worse than the exterior, but it was clean. Cots were piled at one end, and boxes of old clothing and used toys at another. It reeked of stale body odor and simmering onions.

A solidly built man in his fifties wearing a knit cap and sweatshirt came out of what appeared to be an office. He looked as if he'd been a nightclub bouncer in a former life.

"Tobias!" Max made a beeline for him. "Where's Mom?"

Tobias gave Max a clap on the shoulder like an old friend. "She's in the kitchen getting her cut looked at."

"What happened?"

I'd never seen Max look so upset.

"One of the residents went for her with a knife . . . but don't worry—"

"Mom!" Max took off toward the back of the building.

I ran after him, whipping out my cell phone. Maybe I'd need to call for an ambulance.

The back room had been set up as a makeshift soup kitchen, with canned goods and boxes of pasta and cereals neatly arranged on shelves. Sitting on a stack of crates, a slender woman with graying dark hair was trying to wrap a gauze bandage around a wicked cut on her arm. Laugh lines surrounded her blue eyes, which slanted at the corners. Just like her son's.

"Jesus, Mom." Max dropped to his knees in front of her. "What happened?"

Max's mother gave him a wide smile. "Hi, honey. Don't worry, it's not as bad as it looks. Tobias shouldn't have called you for this." Curiously, she regarded me standing in the doorway.

Max took the gauze roll out of his mom's hand and began expertly wrapping her wound. "I should call the cops," he said. "This is assault."

"No, I don't want that. Besides, she's gone." His mother was firm. "You know how junkies behave when they're trying to get clean. She didn't know what she was doing. I've survived worse."

Max smiled wryly at her. "Yeah, I know."

"Besides, we don't need the bad publicity. I'd like to get through one week without having D.C.'s finest pulling up."

"Mom—"

"No, Max. We've talked about this before." Her attention

shifted to me. "Where are your manners? Aren't you going to introduce me?"

"Morgan Abbott," I said without waiting for Max to perform introductions. "I'm pleased to meet you, ma'am."

"Morgan Abbott," she repeated thoughtfully. "You certainly look different in person than you do in the papers."

Eeek. "Thanks, Mrs. Jackson." *I guess.*

"Trisha. We're on a first-name basis around here, despite the knives." She laughed. "Just a little gallows humor. Helps get you through the rough patches."

"Got it, Trisha." I was beginning to like Max's mom.

Max had finished bandaging her arm and stared at her with a look I recognized. Someone was about to get a scathing lecture.

"Could I look around?" I said. "I've never been to a homeless shelter before." I winced. I couldn't have sounded more elitist if I'd been trying.

"Knock yourself out." Trisha stroked her son's head fondly. "Max wants to lecture me, and that's best done in private."

I totally agreed with her.

"Stay close by, Morgan," Max warned. "I need to keep you in visual."

"I will. I'll prop the door open so you can keep me in sight."

God knows I didn't want to add any more stress to his day.

I wandered back out to the main room. Tobias and another volunteer were setting up tables and chairs. "Need some help?" I asked.

"Sure do, mama." Tobias's West Indian accent was cheerful. "You could start by hauling out those chafing trays. Dinner starts in an hour, and once our operating hours begin, they'll be banging the door down."

"So where's everyone now?"

"We close the shelter in the afternoons for cleaning and to discourage loitering."

And knife fights, I added silently.

Eventually I found myself back in the kitchen, chopping carrots, onions, and celery stalks.

Trisha emerged from a back room. Other than the bandage wrapped around the cut on her arm, she seemed like an ordinary soccer mom in a flannel shirt and jeans. "Thanks, Morgan. We really appreciate your help today, since the, uh, incident put us behind schedule."

"No problem, Trisha." I ran a knife through a rib of celery the way I'd seen the sous chefs in Nigel's kitchen do. "I'm having fun. What are we making with this?"

"Alphabet soup. The kids love it, and it gets some vegetables in them. Plus, soup can feed plenty of folks."

"How much does it cost to feed the shelter residents each night?"

"We have a budget of two dollars per person for a meal."

"That's all?" A vending machine candy bar cost two dollars at AOP.

"With food donations and volunteers, we make it happen. We have to. If we don't open our doors, we have kids sleeping on the streets. A newly clean addict might relapse. We're all they have, in some cases."

"Wow."

"It's hard sometimes." Trisha patted her bandaged arm wryly. "But we manage. Never underestimate the power of a safe place to sleep—or alphabet soup!"

I remembered what Nigel told me about the cost of the White House's next banquet—three hundred dollars per person. For one meal.

The disparity was unbelievable.

Trisha began pulling industrial-sized cans of tomatoes from the shelf. "By the way, tell your mother I appreciate all she's tried to do for the urban poor. It's a demographic that doesn't get a lot of attention because they don't vote."

"What do you mean 'tried'?" I asked.

"She introduced legislation to fund a micro-loan program for homeless folks trying to put their lives together. It's amazing what one hundred dollars can buy . . . clothes for a job interview, some dental work." Trisha shrugged. "She wasn't successful, but we appreciate her efforts. Maybe the next congressional session will be different."

I remembered Mom mentioning at the press conference how the opposition party, led by Brittany's dad, Chet Whittaker, killed the micro-loan program. I made a mental note to talk to Mom about it. After she solved the problem of nuclear proliferation in Africa, that is.

Coms buzzing with Secret Service lingo chattered out in the hall. Max entered the kitchen, followed by a female agent I recognized from my father's detail.

The agent's eyes swept the kitchen with the Secret Service once-over. "You brought Tornado here?" she said to Max in an are-you-nuts? tone.

"I wanted to come," I blurted out when Max didn't reply. He'd gone all stoic and agenty like he knew the hammer was going to drop and the only thing he could do was let it conk him on the head. "I made him take me here."

Max winced.

The agent paid no attention to me. She put her hand on the com button. "Tornado's on the move. Bring the Beast up."

"Wait a minute—" I interjected, as the agent began herding me out of the kitchen.

I didn't even get a chance to say good-bye to Trisha because, before I knew it, I was inside the darkened interior of the limo. It drove off. Without Max.

Usually the agents are pretty good about keeping me in the

dark when something was going on. But all the way home I could hear their whispers about Special Agent Jackson's breach of protocol. Procedures had been violated. The president's daughter was placed in a vulnerable situation.

In other words, Max had gotten into serious trouble. Over me. He might be demoted. Or worse—fired.

I felt terrible.

That evening I wandered around the family wing, restless. I flipped on the TV to a cable political show. The two guests were arguing about Mom's Africa policy. The situation there was rapidly getting worse. Innocent people were being slaughtered on both sides. The region was at a standstill. American interests compromised. And all of it was being blamed on my mother for canceling the peace summit.

I wanted to call the show's hotline and tell them that my mom was working her butt off to bring the warring juntas to the table. But they wouldn't be interested in hearing it. Cheap shots and political hit-jobs brought ratings.

Besides, Mom and I had a plan.

I just hoped the "Tornado" didn't wreck Saturday like I always did.

Chapter Twenty

The rest of the week passed in a blur, and Saturday morning Mom woke me super early to get ready for our swap.

I rubbed sleep out of my eyes. "Have you been up all night?"

"Pretty much," she answered. Amazingly, her exhaustion didn't show . . . those youth genes of Grandma Fortescue's were working overtime.

Our plan today was pretty simple: The president (aka me) would remain in the residence wing with the pesky "bug" that had flared up again. Aides would communicate to the president via emails and coms to avoid getting sick.

"I've made notes on last week's legislation agenda," Mom continued. "All you have to do is send them down to Padma throughout the day so it'll seem like you're working, and she'll funnel them to the appropriate staff members for you. It's the same with emails. I draft them and she sends them out.

Humberto will be with me at Camp David, but that's just a quick helicopter ride away if you have a true emergency. If anyone calls—"

"I'll tell them I've just been violently ill and to call tomorrow."

A smile played around Mom's lips. "Maybe you could say you're still feeling unwell and would like to stay in for the day."

Yep, that sounded better.

"By the way, there's a package for you. It arrived last night." Mom handed me a distinctive pink-and-green-striped box from Mimi's boutique. "What did you buy at Mimi's?"

"Nothing, actually." I opened the box. The violet silk minidress lay nestled inside layers of tissue wrap.

Knock 'em dead, said the note on a piece of Mimi's pink stationery.

In all the excitement about going to the homeless shelter, meeting Max's mom, getting him in trouble, *and* tackling the task of impersonating Mom, I totally forgot about the homecoming dance tonight.

What was happening to me? My brain was mush.

I quickly told Mom about the dance and how I'd be going with Konner. "But I can cancel if you need me to. Helping you with the Africa peace accords is way more important."

"Hmm, you're willing to cancel on Konner?" Mom raised a brow. "Actually, I don't think you have to. I should be back from the talks at Camp David in time for you to go to the dance. I need to be at a banquet tonight anyway, and our African guests need to be on their private jets home."

Oh yeah. Tonight was the American Business Leadership Council banquet that Nigel had been slaving over for the last week.

I arranged to meet Mom in the White House residence around six that night, which would give us both plenty of time to get ready for our post-summit parties. Then I headed down to the kitchen. Max had been unusually humorless and by the book with me since the incident at his mom's homeless shelter—well, more by the book than usual—and I hated it. A plan brewed in my head to get us back on friendlier footing.

Nigel had already arrived at the early hour and was organizing the day's prep. "Morgan, bit busy today. Can you get your own breakfast, luv? We've got to melon-ball fifty watermelons by noon for the banquet tonight."

"Of course! As a matter of fact, that's the reason I'm here. Don't worry, I won't get in the way of your staff."

"Are you whipping up your famous blueberry muffins?" asked Maria, the head sous chef.

"Yep."

"*Delicioso*. Save me one, would you?"

I promised I would. Blueberry muffins were my specialty.

I was just pulling a batch out of one of the ovens when Max strode in at the beginning of his shift.

Time to put my plan into action.

"Would you like a muffin?" I asked him sweetly.

Like my mom, Max looked like he had only had about three hours of sleep last night. Unlike my mom, he couldn't hide his exhaustion. He'd nicked himself shaving and his hair was rumpled. In fact, he looked like a college freshman who pulled his first all-nighter. "No, thanks," he answered, and headed to the coffee urn.

Nigel guffawed from the prep table. "You may want to rethink that, mate. Morgan's a bloody good cook."

Rather than argue, Max took a steaming muffin. "Mmm, it is good," he said around a mouthful.

"You sound surprised," I said, amused.

"I am, actually."

"Max, I know I've said this before, but I'm reeeeallly sorry about forcing you to take me to your mom's shelter. Sometimes I get too amped up and forget about the rules."

"It's all right, Morgan. You don't have to apologize for who you are."

"I just wanted to help you out—"

"Morgan, it's not your job to help me with my personal problems. You're my protectee, nothing more. Nothing less."

I stared at him, speechless.

"On Wednesday, I forgot about that," he continued, and scrubbed his face with a weary hand. "But don't worry, it won't happen again. Thanks for the muffin."

He headed out of the kitchen with the half-eaten muffin, probably over to the West Wing and the Secret Service offices down in the basement.

I took a deep breath. I couldn't believe how much his words hurt. I was just a job to him. *Nothing more, nothing less.*

Nigel bumped into me on his way to the walk-in refrigerator with a tray of mini-quiches. "I hate to ask you this, Morgan—"

"I know. You need me out of the way." I surveyed the kitchen. Five chefs labored over an impressive array of ingredients: farm-fresh vegetables, exotic fruits, seafood caught last night and shipped within hours to the White House's provisioning center where it could be inspected for safety and quality. Beef from the Rocky Mountain plains, and quail from a special game farm in Virginia. The pastry chefs were creating a marzipan wonder in the pastry kitchen: a mini rendering of the White House.

I thought about what Max's mother would be serving the residents in her homeless shelter. Some sort of meatless pasta, maybe. Canned peaches if they were lucky.

Escorted up the back stairwell by Max, Hannah arrived an hour later to transform me into Mom. Though no one was supposed to actually see the president today, better safe than sorry. You never knew when an overanxious aide or staff member might burst in unexpectedly, and Abbotts always kept a Plan B in their hip pocket.

We snuck into Mom's bedroom and pulled a couple chairs up to her dust-free, crumb-free desk. Pens and pencils had been placed in a coffee cup that said NO. 1 MOM next to her open laptop computer. Paper clips had their own little tray.

"I should try to get organized," I said. "Then maybe Ms. Gibson wouldn't get on my case so much."

"She does really seem to have it out for you." Hannah picked up a framed photo of me, Mom, and Dad at the Grand Canyon last year. What the photo didn't show was the detail of Secret Service agents standing just outside the shot. "You should send Gibson an email from the president telling her to cut you some slack."

"Yeah!" I activated Mom's laptop with a swipe of my finger— another innovation from Abbott Technology—and played along.

TO: june.gibson@AOP.edu
FROM: s.abbott@whitehouse.gov
SUBJECT: Morgan's grades
Ms. Gibson,
It's come to my attention that my daughter, Morgan, has
been called to your office twice since the beginning of
school for her poor grades. As you know, being the daughter

of the president of the United States can be stressful and can impact her concentration levels. How about you give her a break? I know she'll do her best to get her grades up in future.

Sincerely,

Sara Abbott

President

United States of America

The White House

1600 Pennsylvania Avenue

Washington, D.C.

"Classic!" Hannah crowed. "That would totally scare Gibson."

"I'm not so sure about that." Quickly I deleted the email. "Doesn't seem like much intimidates her. Anyway, I guess I should get to work. I've got a country to run. Time for you to transform me from teen tragedy to world leader."

"As you wish, Madam President." Hannah exaggerated a bow and then broke out her makeup bag and got to work while I sat at Mom's vanity and tried not to grimace at the wig tape Hannah wrapped around my hairline.

"Are you nervous?" Hannah asked as she combed a snarl out of the wig she was about to put on my head.

"Nervous?"

"Yeah, you haven't said a word in over five seconds."

I snorted out a laugh. "Hannah!"

Silence.

"Come on, Morg, give. Something has been bothering you the last couple of days."

"It's nothing. Just . . . Max has been really cold to me ever since the homeless shelter incident." Of course I'd filled Hannah in on the grim details earlier.

Hannah stopped mid-comb. "Really? I thought he was kinda crushing on you."

"Pffft. That was your imagination." *And mine, too,* I added silently.

Hannah shook her head. "No. I'm pretty good about knowing stuff like that. Plus, you don't see how he stares at you when you're not looking."

I squashed a surge of hope. Maybe Max did like me at one point—but that point had passed. He made that clear. I was a job to him. Nothing more. *Nothing less.*

"Let's forget about Max," Hannah said quickly, studying my sad expression. "You've got the awesome power of the presidency at your fingertips, which has got to be way more of a rush than worrying about what some guy thinks of you. What would you do if this gig was yours permanently?"

Hannah was trying her best to make me feel better. *Aww, Hans!* "Okay. If I were president, what would I do . . . I'd twist arms until the micro-loan program for the poor got the votes needed in Congress, for one. Or I'd make the White House feed the people at the homeless shelter instead of the executives of the American Business Leadership Council. Like those guys need another free meal."

"No kidding," Hannah replied. "Half my mom's expense report consists of restaurant tabs she's picked up. I heard her complaining about it yesterday." Both of Hannah's parents were well-connected D.C. lobbyists. Their main occupation consisted of wooing influential powerbrokers.

I pulled Mom's laptop toward me. The screensaver dissolved to the email page I'd opened earlier. "I'd send those fat cat business leaders to the shelter and force them to see how the other half lives." Idly I typed an email under the president's address: "President Abbott requests that the ABLC venue be changed to the Northside Homeless Advocacy Center. . . ."

"Hey, you'd better stop messing around with that," Hannah warned.

I slammed the laptop shut, knowing it would automatically turn off. "You're right. I don't need any trouble today. Let's order a movie. That's something we can do without putting the entire planet on alert!"

I threw on one of Mom's tracksuits and emailed Padma one of the preapproved legislative drafts Mom had worked on last night to keep up the charade that "the president" was upstairs working. Then Hannah and I ordered up a sappy epic love story, which we watched on the flat-screen TV from the comfort of my parents' king-sized bed. The phone rang a couple of times—all incoming calls from the kitchen. It was probably one of Nigel's assistant chefs calling to see what "the president" wanted for lunch, but we were too choked up watching the movie to even think about food. I let Mom's voice mail pick it up.

We were still wiping our eyes as the credits rolled when Mom's phone rang yet again.

"Don't answer it," Hannah sniffled.

"But I have to," I said, catching the name on the LCD screen. I blew my nose. The last three hours had just flown by. "It's Sally Kempton, the communications director. Don't worry, I can handle it."

I cleared my throat and hit the com button. "Sara Abbott here."

"Sara, you're a genius!" Sally's voice sang out over the com. "Moving the ABLC banquet to a homeless shelter is a terrific idea. It will show the American people your strong commitment to your domestic platform, which will offset the hit you've taken over the Africa debacle. You'll go up six points in the polls, at least!"

"Hey, Sally, hold on—"

"I've blasted a media release about tonight, and it's already landed on the afternoon-drive talk radio segments. People are going nuts for this plan!"

What!

My mind jumbled. "But—but how is this possible?"

"Well, Padma did have to work pretty quickly to pull this all off but after she saw your email and sent your message to Nigel Bellingham—"

"My email?"

"Yes. You're still happy with this protocol, aren't you? Padma always copies your drafts to relevant staff members as per your instructions. The kitchen called for clarification until they realized that you were probably knocked out from cold medicine."

All those unanswered phone calls. What had I done?

Sally plowed on, oblivious to my shocked silence. "Nigel wasn't all that crazy about the change, but he spoke to the social secretary about rejiggering the arrangements for tonight at your request. Of course, Clovis didn't *loooove* the idea of moving the banquet to a homeless shelter, either, but she's a pro. They're making it happen."

"Hang on, hang on." I put my hand over the phone's mouthpiece and turned to Hannah, practically frozen in panic. In about one millisecond, I was going to have a total and complete meltdown. Padma sent the draft? I was just fooling around with that email about changing the venue of the ABLC banquet. I didn't mean for Padma to see it, let alone send it out!

Oh god. What was Mom gonna say?

"What's going on?" Hannah mouthed. She'd taken one look at my face and scrambled off the bed to hover next to me.

"I've accidently moved the banquet," I whispered back.

I swallowed despite my dry mouth. "Is there any way we can stop this?" I whispered into the mouthpiece to Sally.

"What's that, Sara? I didn't catch that last bit. Hold on, there's a call coming in for you. It's Trisha Jackson on the line. Do you want to take the call?"

"Well, I—"

In a second, Trisha Jackson's voice entered the line. "This is truly an honor, Madam President. We can't thank you enough for all you're doing to help our residents."

"Uh . . ."

"You know, last week I thought I'd have to close the shelter down for good. Funding just isn't available these days. We've been struggling for so long to keep the doors open. But I believe in miracles."

Think fast, think fast! "You do?"

"What you're doing will increase the profile of the shelter and help us raise more money. It'll keep more families off the streets. Thank you, Madam President. Thank you."

Trisha's voice choked up.

What could I say? *Forget it, Trisha, it's just another horrible mistake courtesy of Morgan Abbott, the biggest screwup in Washington, D.C.?*

Sally got back on the line. "I've got to get this Jackson woman on a media tour ASAP. She'll get you two more percentage points, at least. I'm telling you, Sara, this idea is genius!"

Oh, it was something, all right. But *genius* wasn't the word I'd use.

Somehow I got rid of Sally and hit my mom's private cell phone number with shaky fingers.

The call went straight to voice mail. Humberto's, too. They were probably deep in a delicate negotiation with the African juntas.

I sent Humberto a text message:

CALL ME FASTER THAN WARP SPEED OR I CAN'T BE HELD RESPONSIBLE FOR WHAT IS ABOUT TO HAPPEN TO THE ABLC'S ANNUAL BANQUET.

I couldn't bring myself to leave the same message for Mom. She had enough problems as it was. And she had trusted me not to mess everything up this time. This was a disaster.

"Morgan?" Hannah broke into my thoughts. "You've got a visitor."

Max stood at the door with his hands behind his back, Secret Service–style. Ever the professional. But his words were anything but.

"Morgan. Just what the hell do you think you're doing?"

Chapter Twenty-one

Max entered Mom's suite and shut the door behind him. "Do you have any idea what havoc your antics are causing down below?"

"It's not my fault, Max! It just . . . happened!"

"Just happened? *Just happened?*"

Holy guacamole. Max was livid.

"Calm down, Max—"

"How can I calm down when you basically hijacked a White House function and moved it to my mother's homeless shelter?"

"*She* seems okay with it," I muttered defiantly.

Max's face turned red. "Of course she would! That shelter is her life. I spent half of Wednesday night trying to get her to the emergency room so she could get stitches in her arm, and the other half trying to keep my job—which is to protect YOU!"

He rubbed the back of his neck in agitation. "I almost got

fired because of the breach of protocol. I'm barely hanging on to this detail as it is. I don't need any more problems, Morgan."

Oh.

"C'mon, Max." I had to lighten the atmosphere between us. "Moving the banquet to your mom's shelter can't be that bad. Think of all the good we're doing."

I actually thought the blood vessel pulsing in his neck might pop. "Let me break it down for you, Morgan," he said with exaggerated patience. "The Secret Service has gone into level-four action to sweep the Northside Homeless Advocacy Shelter for tonight's unscheduled event. Normally it takes at least forty-eight hours to secure a location for the president! The kitchen is in an uproar and half the chefs want to quit. The White House butler is having a nervous breakdown because he was just informed that the banquet he and his staff have worked for over A WEEK to set up in the East Room—complete with Kennedy AND Eisenhower china—is being moved to a run-down homeless shelter."

I started to hyperventilate.

"Chill out, Max," Hannah interjected. "She didn't mean for this to happen."

"Of course she didn't," Max said sardonically. "She never means for anything crazy to happen to her. It just does. No wonder she's gone through three different agent details in the past year."

Ouch. That hurt. But what could I say? It was true.

"Maybe it'll all work out," I managed to squeak out. "I think your mom is amazing. So is the work she does."

Max made a visible effort to calm himself. "She is amazing. But *my* mom isn't brokering a secret peace deal between two warring African military juntas while trying to prevent nuclear proliferation. That plan is in jeopardy now because you're leaving The Bubble to go to my mother's shelter, where you could be exposed for impersonating the president."

"Mom should be back by then," I started, but my explanation was cut short by the buzz of the presidential com. "It's Humberto," I said, glancing at the LCD screen. "Thank god. I'll get him to put the kibosh on the whole thing."

Easier said than done. Humberto told me to hold tight until he got back from Camp David. By the time he arrived at Mom's suite, it seemed like he'd aged about twenty years since that morning.

"Okay, let's go into damage-control mode." Humberto checked his BlackBerry and ticked down the list of events for the night with the stylus. "Plan A is to cancel the event—"

YESSSSS.

"—which we can't do because all the major cable networks and C-SPAN will be covering it live. If we cancel, it'll look like you—I mean, your mother—doesn't really care about the homeless. The talking point on the Sunday political chat shows will be that the whole thing was a diversion to distract from the president's failure to broker a deal between General Mfuso and Bishop Welak."

NOOOO.

Humberto pecked at the screen of his BlackBerry again with an air of someone used to putting out fires. "Plan B is to roll with it. We have no choice. We've rescheduled the press conference for after the dinner to give Sara plenty of time to get up to speed."

Humberto snapped his PDA shut and headed to the door. "But your mom is running late so you'll have to impersonate her for the first hour or so until she gets there. And you better be pretty convincing tonight because if word of this swap leaks, at the very least it'll be the end of your mother's administration and her political career."

Yikes.

"I'll be ready," I said to his back with more confidence than I felt.

"Let's hope so." Humberto swept out of the room.

Hannah draped an arm around my shoulder. "Don't stress, Morgan. You can do it. I know you can. Plus I'm gonna make the president look kick-ass tonight."

I hugged her back. "Thanks, Hannah. But not too kick-ass. Remember, it's my mom we're talking about."

"Trust me. I can make a boring power suit look fly." She

headed into the walk-in closet muttering something about blue blouses with brown suits, leaving me alone with Max.

The silence grew pretty loud between us. Finally I couldn't take it anymore. "Say something."

"Like what?"

"I don't know. Yell at me some more about how much I screw everything up. About how this plan is never going to work. That I've put my mother's political career in jeopardy. Anything."

Max sighed heavily before running his hand through his hair in a way that made my stomach tingle. "I should yell at you some more . . . but I can't."

"You can't?"

"No. Because in truth, I think you're a pretty amazing person."

"I'm . . . what?"

Max had been gazing at me with a slight smile. "Despite the fact that you drive me completely nuts and are the biggest security challenge in the entire Secret Service detail, I have to tell you that I really admire what you're doing."

Warmth crept through me. "You do?"

"Absolutely. You're helping your mom bring peace to Africa. And despite your antics, you're helping my mom feed the homeless."

He came right up to me. "I'm proud to be the one protecting you, Morgan. Even if you're a walking disaster sometimes."

I gave a shaky laugh. Max's long eyelashes swept down over his blue eyes. I leaned in. *He's going to kiss me*, I thought.

His com chirped and the soft expression on his face disappeared as he stepped back. "Jackson here," he said into his wireless mouthpiece.

My heart was booming against my chest.

He turned back to me and I thought for a moment he was going to talk about what almost happened. He didn't. "Come on, Morgan, it's showtime. You need to get ready."

187

Chapter Twenty-two

Due to the miracle of the White House staff's professionalism, when the guests arrived at the South Portico for the banquet they were whisked off in a fleet of buses to the Northside Homeless Advocacy Center as if the whole thing had been planned for months.

The guests—members of Congress, titans of American industry—had dressed in their best for a White House banquet. I tried not to think how funny they would look milling around Trisha's shabby building in their expensive business suits and couture dresses, rubbing shoulders with the homeless. The president must keep a straight face in every situation. Even the hilarious ones.

After I texted Konner that I'd be late to the dance and I'd catch up with him later (he wasn't as bummed as I thought he'd be), I'd arrived at the homeless shelter in the Big Beast, aka the seven-car presidential motorcade, early to avoid having to make a grand entrance. Secret Service agents had set up a security station at the entrance and were sweeping guests with metal detectors.

I steered clear of a huge floral arrangement of my mom's signature white lilies displayed at the end of the buffet table. I'd forgotten that the social secretary made sure lilies were present at President Abbott's off-site events—that is, the ones that I wouldn't be attending. The last thing I needed was the disaster of a runny nose and itchy eyes to complicate my impersonation of Mom.

After "meeting" Trisha Jackson (she was over the moon) as the president, I insisted I help serve the buffet, mostly because I didn't want to talk to anyone of importance, like the speaker of the house and my dad's business partners. Humberto agreed. Not only was it a prudent move, but it had the advantage of being a terrific photo op. Behind the safety of chafing trays, I dished up Nigel's jerked pulled pork to an array of street people and gussied-up guests.

The shelter regulars didn't look all that pleased with their new dinner guests. I suppose they didn't appreciate the metal detectors or the security searches, either. They seemed to keep to themselves and many opted to take their trays to a private dining room Trish had set up for those guests who preferred to eat in peace.

Humberto hovered discreetly behind me, just in case any

awkward situations cropped up. One did, in the shape of the opposition leader, Chet Whittaker, who came to my station for a splat of Caribbean coleslaw to go on his biodegradable plate.

"Clever idea," he drawled in his southern accent. "No one would suspect this is a political stunt." An easy smile showed his capped teeth.

Humberto leaned toward me to whisper an appropriate reply, but without waiting, I said: "Well, if you'd quit blocking my micro-loan initiative for the poor, I wouldn't have to resort to 'stunts.'" I smiled sweetly, too. "Chet."

Humberto's jaw clicked shut. Congressman Whittaker got the hint and moved on. I wouldn't let Brittany's dad intimidate me any more than his daughter did.

The volume inside the echoey building rose, and I couldn't help grinning when I saw Tobias and the CEO of Wall Street's biggest hedge fund arguing good-naturedly. Trisha was running around making contacts. Max watched his mom fondly for a moment before he caught my eye.

It was going to be okay, the look said. We were going to get through this. He smiled at me.

I returned the smile and fought a quivery feeling.

As I tried to get my heart to beat normally again, I heard a familiar high-pitched voice, whining a little distance away from me.

"What *is* this? Paper plates? Plastic forks? I thought I was going to the White House for dinner, not charity time at the soup kitchen. Ugh, I hope I don't get a communicable disease."

Brittany Whittaker. Cripes.

And like the spoiled brat that she was, she never shut up. "Ew, that man over there has no front teeth! This place stinks and I think I saw a cockroach. God, I can't believe I'm going to be late for homecoming because of this. You owe me big time, Daddy."

"Simmer down, sugar." Congressman Whittaker turned a shade of cooked salmon when he realized I'd overheard his daughter's griping. He laughed uncomfortably. "Heh, that's teenage girls for you, eh, Madam President? They think the world revolves around them. I'm sure you understand, given that you have a daughter the same age as my Brittany."

I probably should have smiled and agreed with Congressman Whittaker. Yesiree, looking back on the moment, I should have kept it zipped and maybe everything would have turned out differently.

But instead I said, "Well, Chet, my daughter, Morgan, might be the same age as Brits, but she wouldn't dream of insulting her hosts with an inflated sense of entitlement."

Brittany's mouth hung open wide enough to expose the piece of gum she'd been smacking. Congressman Whittaker's brows rose up to meet the front of his hairpiece. "Brits?" he said.

Uh-oh . . .

I tried to cover. "Yes, isn't that your nickname in school, Brittany? At least that's what my daughter calls you. She talks about you all the time."

"She does?" Brittany's face brightened as she flashed her signature suck-up smile. "Morgan talks about me? With *you*?"

"She says she really admires your . . . political skills," I fibbed.

I glanced around desperately and caught Humberto's eye. *Help!*

He hurried over. "Important phone call for you, Madam President. You should take it immediately."

I gave the Whittakers an apologetic smile. "Duty calls," I said, and got the heck out of there.

"Thanks, Humberto." I sighed in relief.

"Yeah, yeah." But he grinned at me.

Max approached in the quick-casual way that Secret Service agents train for six months in order to perfect. I didn't like the look on his face. "Foxfire's detail just called."

Foxfire. Mom's Secret Service code name.

"The talks went on longer than expected," Max said, listening carefully into his earpiece. "They've left Camp David but they're running late."

"Well, that's a good sign, isn't it?" Elation raced through me. Mom was going to pull off the biggest challenge of her administration. *GO, MOM!*

Humberto and Max exchanged glances. "It means that you're going to have to deliver the press briefing," Humberto said.

"You're kidding, right?" I kept waiting for Max to say, "Yeah, just kidding."

But he didn't.

I rubbed my left ear, Mom-style. "Did anyone see the white-chocolate gingersnaps?" I asked, changing the subject.

"You've certainly perfected your impersonation of the president," Humberto remarked wryly, handing me a BlackBerry with some notes for the press conference.

"I sure hope so," I muttered.

"I brought someone in to help you," Max said. "We need her expertise if this is to be successful."

I turned. "Hannah!" I cried, about to throw my arms around her, but then I remembered who I was impersonating. I extended my hand instead.

"Hey, now!" Hannah shook my hand all formal-like. "I heard someone's going to give a press conference to be broadcast from coast to coast. I'll get you camera ready."

"Thanks, Hannah. I know you're missing out on the homecoming dance."

"Pfft. Don't worry about it. That's what friends are for."

Over Hannah's shoulder, I saw Brittany Whittaker eyeing the two of us suspiciously. Then she started toward us.

Without thinking, I shrank behind the buffet table.

Big. Mistake.

In all the excitement, I'd forgotten to tell Humberto to get rid of the lily displays. Immediately, itchiness prickled my eyes and my nose started running like crazy. Oh geez, this was the last thing I needed right now!

"What the—" Hannah flinched as I blasted a sneeze.

A couple of shelter residents inched away.

"Hannah—help!" I felt my eye makeup running down my cheeks. Another violent sneeze, and the jig would be up.

"Bathroom." Hannah firmly steered me away from the buffet.

Through the watery haze of my allergy-induced tears, I caught sight of Brittany watching us.

Chapter Twenty-three

Panic exploded through me while Max, under Hannah's direction, cleared the shelter's closetlike (and let's be honest, smelly) bathroom for presidential use. He set the Secret Service detail to guard the door while he fetched Hannah's makeup kit.

"Brittany knows I'm not the president." I mopped my nose with a wad of industrial-grade toilet paper. "She *knows*!"

"Morgan, maintain." Hannah took me by the shoulders and gave me a shake. "Brittany Whittaker doesn't know jack. Her teeny tiny mind can't handle anything more complicated than gossip and brownnosing."

"Yeah, but being evil is second nature to her. She knows I'm the one allergic to lilies, not my mom."

"She's not going to put two and two together. And if she did, she'd come up with five."

I spluttered out a reluctant laugh.

"Even if she did figure it out," Hannah went on, "what's she going to do? Who'd believe her? She'd look like an idiot if she ran around claiming that you were impersonating your mother. I'm in on the secret, and I don't even believe it sometimes."

I began to calm down. Hannah made perfect sense. Right. Who would believe Brittany anyway?

A few seconds later, Max arrived with Hannah's makeup kit. "The press conference is set," he said through the cracked door. "We're just waiting for the president."

"Tell them I'll be there in ten minutes." Mentally I shoved Brittany out of my head and reviewed the talking points Humberto had given me, thankful that I'd gotten used to memorizing lines on the fly from drama class. *Concentrate, Morgan!* I needed to pull off this press briefing and the biggest role of my life. So much was at stake: my mom's secret peace mission; our swapped identities; a chance to breathe life into Mom's micro-loan initiative, which would give Trisha Jackson the tools to help those who needed it most.

It all hinged on this press conference.

It all hinged on the Tornado.

I emerged from the bathroom, freshly made up.

Humberto met me at the door. "Don't forget to link the micro-loan program to your mom's domestic platform."

"Okay—"

"Try to get a mention in about urban health-care centers."

"Got it."

"Close with your mom's slogan."

"Check."

I headed to my Secret Service detail, waiting to lead me to the stage.

"And don't forget to breathe!" Humberto hissed after me.

At his prompting, I took a big breath. Feverishly, I reviewed the talking points one more time and tried not to remember the disaster I made of my last big speech in front of the senior class. Wig on tight. Smile of confidence plastered on my face. Heart pounding like a drum. Check, check, and check.

The back half of the shelter had been roped off for the press briefing. A small stage complete with flags and a podium stood under the glare of temporary stage lights. Chairs for the press lined the floor in front of the stage, but the banquet guests—rich and poor alike—gathered around to hear "my" speech.

Led by Max, a team of Secret Service agents cleared a path through the gathering for my entrance.

Adrenaline gushed through me as I took the stage.

Like Mom says: showtime.

"Thank you all," I said once the applause died down. I remembered to cock my head to the side.

"You may have wondered about the change in venue for the White House's annual tribute to the American Business Leadership Council."

My eyes swept the crowd. Heads nodded. Some vigorously.

Some really vigorously.

Over by stage left, Humberto uncharacteristically chewed at a thumbnail.

"Sometimes seeing is believing," I continued. "And I believe we've neglected to see what has been right under our noses. Homelessness. Hunger. Right here in the richest nation on earth, and in the shadow of political power.

"I've been trying to address the inequalities in our great nation. Micro-loan programs, grants for children in poverty, urban health-care centers, these initiatives have long been the cornerstone of my administration. But the other day, someone opened my eyes to the fact that I haven't been doing enough."

I let the moment hang.

"Trisha Jackson, the director of this amazing program, and countless other unsung heroes, have shown that it isn't enough to propose solutions, and I hope that others will agree. Solutions take action. And solutions take partnerships with people who can help. That's why you're here today."

The audience went really quiet. I prayed that was a good sign.

"I hope now that you've met some of the residents of this shelter, you see that people are as great an investment as a stock IPO or a takeover buyout."

I lifted my right hand and stabbed the air in front to me to make my point. It was totally a Mom thing to do.

"My motto has always been that change starts with one person, and one person only. Today, change starts with you. I hope you will join me in transforming our country. For the better."

Sweat tickled under my wig. No one was saying anything. Maybe they'd seen through my disguise. Maybe I'd given myself away somehow.

A crash of applause made me jump out of my skin. In amazement I watched as crusty reporters took notes feverishly. The guests behind them were applauding. Trisha Jackson held a tissue to her nose while Tobias patted her shoulder.

Hannah was doing a happy dance over by the buffet table. I glanced at Humberto. He was nodding, pleased. Thankfully, the queasy expression on his face had vanished.

Max. My eyes found his.

The smile he gave me rocked me down to my socks.

I remembered Dad's rule: Leave them wanting more. I stepped away from the podium—*phew!*—and hurried into the protective cocoon of my Secret Service detail, leaving Humberto to field more questions from journalists. The detail whisked me away from the stage.

I wasn't really sure where we were going. The adrenaline had worn off, and I started trembling. Blindly I let the detail, headed up by Max, guide me to the next staging area.

Which was . . . the stinky bathroom again.

A homeless person in a rank trench coat and floppy hat slouched against the door.

"Excuse us," Max said firmly. "We need to secure the area."

The homeless person raised her head.

"Mom!"

"Shhhh, honey. Let's step inside where we'll have some privacy. Agent Jackson will make sure no one disturbs us." Mom nodded at Max, who ushered us both inside the bathroom.

I wanted another one of Max's rare smiles, but he'd gone all hard-core agent again, stern expression and hard eyes. Maybe I'd imagined that awesome look he'd given me at the end of my speech.

Once inside the bathroom, Mom hugged me hard. "You were wonderful, Morgan. I think you've given the best speech of my administration."

"Really?" A glow of pride lit me up.

"Hijacking a presidential banquet and moving it to a homeless shelter is not the way I would have handled it, but your crazy plan may have just saved my micro-loan initiative. After tonight's news cycle, Congress would be foolish not to sign the micro-loan legislation. How did all this happen, anyway?"

"It's a long story. Let's just say the Tornado strikes again." I pulled off the wig and Mom rumpled my hair.

"Morgan Abbott, politics might be in your future. After all, we're cut from the same cloth."

"Awww, thanks, Mom." We beamed at each other. "How'd the peace talks go?"

"Really well. Not only did General Mfuso agree to deliver the yellowcake uranium to the U.N.'s International Atomic Energy Agency, they're also one step closer to holding democratic elections. I'll have another important announcement to make. Might as well do it now, since the press is already here." Mom began unbuttoning the trench coat. "Ready to become Morgan Abbott again?"

"So ready." I did a double take when Mom shrugged out of the coat. "Is that Mimi's purple silk mini?" I gasped.

"Sure is. I thought since we're swapping, you should get ready for your homecoming dance."

"But I thought—"

"You'll have time to make it, sweetie. We'll get the sirens and flashing lights going on the motorcade so you're not stuck in traffic."

"Mom! Isn't that taking presidential prerogatives too far? You always said we should be careful not to throw our weight around this town."

"I think you've earned a little weight-throwing tonight." Mom slipped into her suit and fluffed her hair. "I'll send for Hannah. You two stay here and get ready for the dance. Humberto is arranging for additional time with the press outside the shelter so I can announce the African peace deal. It'll be a perfect time for you two to sneak away."

She encircled me in another a big hug. "I'm really proud of you, Morgan."

I hugged her back. We *did* make a good team.

"Back at ya, Mom."

Chapter Twenty-four

Hannah snuck into the bathroom under Secret Service cover, and she and I got ready for the homecoming dance. By the time she threaded neon-pink hair extensions into my flattened hair, I began to feel like myself again. The violet silk mini also worked wonders.

"I hope Konner won't be mad that I'm super late for the dance," I said.

"Guess he'll have to learn to deal. Now hold still." Hannah carefully settled a line of false eyelashes on my lid and blew the glue dry. "When I'm done, no one will ever suspect that a half hour ago, you were the president of the United States."

"Thank gawd." I waited until Hannah finished gluing the other eye with false lashes. "I couldn't have pulled it off without you, Hans. I know it's hard to be my friend sometimes."

"What are you talking about?"

"Well, all the paparazzi issues, and, uh, me impersonating

the president, and hanging with someone continually on academic probation—"

"Hang on, who hooked me up with Prince Richard— helloooo? And who makes me laugh basically every day I'm with her? And is the nicest person I know? Yeah, real punishment, Morgan."

We grinned at each other.

"Thanks for being there for me," I said.

"That's what BFFs are for," she replied. "Now back to important business."

Hannah's mad skills with makeup transformed me into a vixen with smoky eyes. She made herself look super killer in a scarlet jersey number she'd pulled out of her Louis Vuitton travel bag—wrinkle-free fabric, she explained. She twisted bandeaus through her hair and dusted us both with a hint of body glitter.

I regarded us in the scratched mirror. We looked awesome.

"Let's go get our dance on," I said to her, excitement bubbling up. I was soooo ready to cut loose on the dance floor. Freedom!

Max's jaw loosened when we emerged from the shelter's bathroom. This time I could feel myself blushing.

"You look . . ." He cleared his throat. "Beautiful."

We stared at each other for a couple of heartbeats.

Max seemed to mentally shake himself. He got back on track and the detail swept us out of the shelter.

"Not bad, sistah," Hannah whispered to me.

"What are you talking about?" I asked innocently.

"You know what I'm talking about. You're making Max's job hard."

I guess I didn't think of it that way.

Out front, journalists and camera crews surrounded Mom and peppered her with questions.

"—when did the breakthrough between the Mfuso and Welak juntas occur—"

"—will there be a formal announcement of the cease-fire soon—"

"—what sort of aid will the U.S. render to the war-torn area—"

Mom held up her hand and the journalists quieted. "A formal announcement will be made tomorrow, but yes, a cease-fire between General Mfuso and the Democratic People's Army has been agreed upon. The secretary of state will provide details on the negotiations. It's not a solution, but it's progress."

What Dad calls journo-flurry erupted again, with more questions being thrown at Mom.

Mom had called an end to the questions and was beginning to ease away from the bank of microphones. Brittany Whittaker stepped out of the shadows of the shelter, a big bouquet of those horrible lilies in her arms. With a plastered smile, she asked Parker, my mom's Secret Service agent, if she could give them to my mother.

"Sure," Mom said when Parker started to shake his head. "You're one of Morgan's classmates, aren't you?"

"Yes, I am," Brittany said. Then her sugary voice changed. "But YOU are not the president, you're—*Morgan Abbott*."

Her manicured talons reached out and yanked my mom's hair.

Max says that Secret Service agents are trained to tackle first, ask questions later. I couldn't really get a good look at Brittany under a dog pile of agents and the blinding flash of a thousand cameras capturing this particular Kodak moment.

"Did I just dream that?" I asked Hannah as we entered the Baby Beast.

She was laughing so hard, I thought we were going to have to hospitalize her. "If that was a dream, don't wake me up."

I regarded the swarm of camera crews jostling to get a photo of Brittany down on the ground. "I guess *she'll* find out tomorrow that not all publicity is good publicity."

"Karma, baby. Karma."

Chapter twenty-five

We cut through the traffic knotted around Dupont Circle and the never-ending gridlock on K Street with the presidential motorcade in full-on siren mode. Konner wasn't answering his cell, but that didn't surprise me. He'd be in his element at the homecoming dance, hanging with his buds, basking in his popularity. I sent him a text message and hoped he'd check it before I got there.

We arrived at the front doors of the Academy of the Potomac's gym an hour late.

Max professionally cleared a zone around the car door, shooing away the people who were trying to gawk at the interior of the Baby Beast (no, we don't have a microwave oven or a rocket launcher inside presidential limos) before he helped Hannah and me out of the car.

Konner was nowhere to be seen.

But surprisingly I wasn't disappointed at all. Only slightly ticked off. I mean, Konner had made such a big deal about taking me to the dance. The least he could do was meet me at the door.

Inside the gym, Brittany's decorating committee had gone a bit over the top. It looked like the colors pink and purple had thrown up in there. Petals from wilted flowers dribbled over the gym floor, where they were stomped to pitiful brown bits. Colored gels over the lights turned everyone's skin an insane shade of green and yellow.

"Whoa. I think Alice got lost on her way down the rabbit hole," Hannah said over the music pumping through the gym's loudspeakers. "Too bad Brits isn't here. She'd really enjoy how she's made the whole school look like they have impetigo." She pointed to a group of classmates gathered around a cell phone replaying a downloaded video of the president's press conference at the point when Brittany got tackled to the ground. "I'm not sure she'd like that very much, though."

"Max says they took her down to the Central Detention Facility," I said.

"The D.C. jail? Wow," Hannah said.

"The Secret Service doesn't mess around if you attack the president. But I'm sure Congressman Whittaker will spring her pretty quickly."

The music switched to a slow song. Couples jostled and rearranged into clusters.

Leaving me a clear view of Konner draped all over Mya, the head cheerleader.

He held her hips and the two of them slowly swayed. She didn't seem to mind the way his eyes were locked on her boobs, which mounded over the edge of her low neckline.

Someone nudged him and whispered in his ear. He sprang away from Mya so fast she stumbled. "Pig!" she yelled as he sauntered toward me.

"Hey, babe." Konner raised his arms all gangsta, then lowered them around my shoulders. "I've been waiting forever for you to show up. I missed you."

Hannah rolled her eyes. "Ugh. I feel my dinner coming up. I'll catch you later, Morgan."

"Okay, Hannah." I pushed Konner away. "So you've been missing me?"

"Yeah. Hey, I hope you're not getting the wrong idea about Mya. She felt bad for me because you were late."

"So she was just being nice."

Konner gave me one of his lopsided grins. "Yeah. Being nice." He lowered his mouth to mine, but I jerked away.

Puzzlement glimmered on his brow. "Don't get mad, babe. Look, I got you a corsage and everything because you're so special to me."

He opened his suit jacket and pulled out a crushed corsage.

Lilies.

My abused nose began tickling immediately. "Get those things away from me."

"Why? I thought all girls liked flowers."

"Because I'm allergic to lilies, Konner! Ahhhhh—" I let loose a huge sneeze. I took the corsage and threw it at his chest.

"Man, Morgan, why are you getting so worked up?"

I gave a disbelieving laugh. "You don't know me at all. You've never even tried to get to know me. The only thing I am to you is the president's daughter. A trophy, not a girlfriend. I see that now."

"Hey. Don't go mental just because I forgot you have an allergy. I can't be expected to remember everything about you."

"We're finished, Konner. And this time it's for good." I spun around and began walking away.

"Oh yeah?" Konner called after me. "Well, I've had enough of you and your mind games, Morgan Abbott. It's over."

"Whatever."

I reached Max, who had stationed himself by the doorway as usual. I didn't have to say anything to him. I realized now that I never had to say anything to Max. He always understood.

"Ready, Morgan?" Max held his elbow out and I took it.

"Yes. Take me home, Max."

"You got it."

I sent Hannah a text message from the limo:

i'm outtie text when u want limo to p/u up

    ok wat about Konner?

it's over

    u ok?

i'm better than ok—talk tomorrow, ya?

    ya. g'nite

nite ☺

Max said nothing as the sparkly Washington skyline slipped past. I knew we had to talk, but right now, I just needed to think. So much had happened in the past few weeks, I felt like a different Morgan Abbott. Maybe I grew up a little. Maybe I learned that I could handle whatever life as the nation's First Daughter could dish out.

Back at the White House, quiet hushed along the corridors. Most of the staff was still detailed at the media event at Trisha Jackson's homeless shelter, while Mom was putting in some overtime with the secretary of state to implement the peace accords she'd hammered out with the African military juntas.

I was sitting in my room when my cell phone chirped. A text message appeared:

Meet me in the East Room

Max. It had to be.

Feeling breathless and tingly all at the same time, I ran barefoot down the Cross Hall's red-and-gold carpet, still wearing the violet silk mini. Portraits of Jimmy Carter and Gerald Ford gazed down at me, and I wondered if my mother's portrait would eventually hang between one of the neoclassical pillars. The first female president in two and a half centuries of male presidents.

That was gonna be awesome.

At the entrance to the East Room, I patted the marble head of President Lincoln sitting atop an obsidian pillar. "What do you think, Abe? Did Mom and I pull it off today?"

"I think *you* pulled it off."

I jumped clean out of my skin. "Max!"

He was leaning against the doorway to the East Room. He'd taken off his tie and unbuttoned his collar, and his hair stood up in a way that made my heart stutter just a teensy bit. Okay, a lot.

"I want to talk to you," he said.

My heart switched into overdrive.

Next to the Red Room, the East Room was my favorite. The room was huge. Mom hosted major events here: concerts, balls, banquets. Gold wallpaper coated the walls, and matching gold drapes swagged over the tall windows overlooking the South Lawn. I used to Rollerblade across the parquet floors until the White House usher put a stop to it after I crashed into the priceless Steinway piano and left a *barely noticeable* dent on one of the legs.

Tables from the aborted ABLC banquet had been pushed against the wall, leaving the floor in the middle of the room cleared. The crystal chandeliers had been dimmed to a romantic glow.

"What's that music?" I asked when I heard the sounds of a slow pop song drift through the room.

"I'm sorry you had to leave your homecoming dance early," Max said.

"Don't be. I'm not sorry."

"So you and Konner . . . ?"

"Finished."

Max smiled his rare smile. And it was even more devastating than one of Konner's. It lit his whole face up, and I knew this smile was genuine.

"Dance with me?"

I hesitated. "Won't you get in trouble? I thought Secret Service agents weren't supposed to 'fraternize with their protectees.'"

"I'm not your Secret Service agent anymore."

My heart, which had been pounding against my chest, stalled. "Did you say you're not my agent anymore?" Crap! What had I done?

"Yep." He drew me in his arms, and began to circle with me in a slow step.

Good lord. I'd forgotten how great Max slow-danced.

I tried to stay cool. "I'm really sorry if I got you in trouble again, Max."

"Morgan—"

"I'll get your job back, I promise."

"Morgan—"

"I'll talk to my mom. . . ."

"I wasn't fired." Max's head came a little closer to mine. "I asked to be reassigned."

I swallowed hard. "Why?"

"Because—" He tilted my head up. "I'd rather be your boyfriend than your bodyguard."

Let me just state for the record, right here, right now. Max Jackson kissed better than he danced.

And you can quote me.